BLUE SKIN
OF THE SEA

ALSO AVAILABLE FROM
LAUREL-LEAF BOOKS

ALSO BY
GRAHAM SALISBURY

GRAHAM SALISBURY

BLUE SKIN OF THE SEA

A NOVEL IN STORIES

Published by Laurel-Leaf
an imprint of Random House Children's Books
a division of Random House, Inc.
New York

This is a work of fiction. Names, characters, places, and incidents
either are the product of the author's imagination or are used fictitiously.
Any resemblance to actual persons, living or dead, events, or
locales is entirely coincidental.

Originally published in hardcover in the United States by
Delacorte Press, New York, in 1992. This edition published by
arrangement with Delacorte Press.

Laurel-Leaf and colophon are registered trademarks
of Random House, Inc.

www.randomhouse.com/teens

Educators and librarians, for a variety of teaching tools,
visit us at www.randomhouse.com/teachers

RL: 5.5
ISBN: 978-0-440-21905-7
March 2007
Printed in the United States of America
22 21 20 19 18 17 16 15 14

For Robyn, Sandi, Miles, Ashley, Melanie, Alex, and Keenan. And, of course, Anno, Pato, Carol, Rex, and Loriann.

"When you cannot find peace in yourself it is useless to look for it elsewhere."

La Rochefoucauld

Many thanks to my good friends and mentors: William Melvin Kelley, Diane Lefer, Pamela Painter, Gladys Swan, Wendy Lamb, Emilie Jacobson, and Marian Biscay, with a special note of gratitude to Alex Haley, whose extraordinary book, *Roots*, transformed me into a voracious lifetime reader.

Contents

Deep Water

(1953)

A noon-high Hawaiian sun poured over the jungled flanks of the Big Island, spreading down into the village of Kailua-Kona and the blistering metal bed of Uncle Harley's fish truck. Keo and I sat across from each other on black rubber inner tubes that Uncle Harley, Keo's father, had gotten for us at the Chevron station in Holualoa. It was so hot you could lick your finger and make wet lines on the tubes, then watch them disappear in a matter of seconds.

I'd wanted to stay up at the house with Aunty Pearl, where it was cooler, and shoot cardboard boxes with Keo's new BB gun. But Keo wanted to go down to the harbor with Uncle Harley and go swimming. "And if you don't come with me," he said, "I'll *never* let you shoot the BB gun."

Uncle Harley pulled up under a grove of palm trees at the far end of the village, where the pier was. Before the truck had even stopped, Keo leaped out and raced through the trees to the small, sandy cove on the back side of the pier. He ran into the ocean until he fell, then swam out to deep water.

I threw the tubes out of the truck and ran down behind him, but held back when the water reached my waist.

Uncle Harley backed the truck out of the trees and started to drive out onto the pier. Then he stopped, and yelled. "Hey! You boys stay in the shallow part." But Keo had gone under. The glassy water barely rippled where he had been.

"Sonny," Uncle Harley said, scowling down at me. "Tell him to stay in the shallow part." He shook his head and drove away.

I stared at the spot where I'd last seen Keo, waiting for him to surface. The wide rock and concrete pier stretched off to my left, then elbowed out toward open sea, just past a small boat landing on the cove side. Dad's small skiff dozed at its mooring a short distance out.

Keo finally popped up far from where he'd gone under. "Come on," he yelled. "It's fun out here." When I didn't move he made chicken sounds, yelling *"buk-buk-bu-gock!"* and pretending to flap a pair of wings.

He knew I was afraid of deep water. At seven, Keo was fearless. Dad was like that, too, and I wanted to be like them so much my head hurt just thinking about it. It just came to them naturally, like breathing. I was chicken, just like Keo said. But why? I tried and tried and tried. I was six, only a year younger than Keo, and I still couldn't swim.

"*Kay*-o, *Kay*-o, what do you *say*-o," I yelled back. Uncle Raz sometimes said that, and Keo didn't like it.

I waded out to shoulder depth and copied the way Keo swam, like a dog, only I stayed close to the beach in water just shallow enough to kick the bottom with one foot whenever I started to sink.

Keo swam in to shore and ran up to get the tubes, his

glistening back several shades darker than mine, because his mother, Aunty Pearl, had Hawaiian blood. I was Portuguese-French.

Keo brought both tubes back and ringed one out to me. I dropped it over my head and hooked my arms over an inner curve, then followed Keo out into the cove toward the small boat landing. With the tubes we were equals, and for the moment I splashed along beside him, forgetting Uncle Harley's warning to stay in the shallows.

"Hey." Keo pointed to the opening between the pier and the end of the breakwater.

Dad's small, blue and orange sampan disappeared on the far side of the pier. Its old diesel engine *tok-tok-tok-tokked* slowly into the harbor, sounding slightly muffled when it slipped from view.

My heart thumped against the tube. Even then, six years into my life, Dad was still a mystery, a quiet shadowy man. I saw him every afternoon when the boats came in, but I didn't really know him. I didn't even *live* with him because my mother had died when I was a baby. I lived with Keo and his parents, my Aunty Pearl and Uncle Harley.

I started back to shore to go out on the pier, following Keo. Why had Dad come in so early? I stopped kicking and let the tube drift. If Dad had seen us in the deep part, I'd be in for it.

"Wait," I said.

"What?"

"Let's go catch crabs on the rocks."

"What for? Let's go to the boat."

"Naah, more fun to catch crabs."

Keo scowled at me, but he turned and kicked over toward the rocks anyway.

A half hour later Dad buzzed into the cove in his skiff, his sampan cleaned and moored in the bay. He shut the engine down and let the skiff glide in to the beach, tilting the outboard up so the propeller wouldn't scrape the sand.

Keo slogged through the shallows and caught the bow. "Take us for a ride, Uncle Raymond."

"Not today, Keo. Sonny and I have something to do."

Dad smiled at me. "We're going swimming."

Out of the corner of my eye, I saw Keo look over at me, but I pretended not to notice.

"But Uncle Raymond," Keo said. "Sonny can't swim. He's *chicken*." I glanced up at Dad, then looked away when our eyes met.

"There was a time, Keo, when you were chicken, too," Dad said. His words were sharp, like fishhooks. "Go play by yourself for a while—we'll be back in an hour or so."

Keo stared at Dad, his mouth slightly open. Neither of us had ever heard Dad sound so angry. It took a lot to get him upset.

Dad threw me the small orange life preserver I always wore in the skiff. "Put this on," he said.

I climbed into the boat and sat in the center seat. Dad's fins and face mask were under the rear seat beside the glass-bottom box he'd made for me, my window to the ocean floor.

"Keo, push us out," Dad said.

Keo gave the skiff a shove and watched it glide away from the beach. Dad lowered the engine, then pulled the cord easily and kicked it over in one short motion.

As we moved out of the cove, I glanced back and watched Keo race out to the end of the pier. When we broke into the harbor Keo watched us like a puppy, pacing, then stopping, then pacing again.

My father was a fisherman, as his father had been. And before him, Great-grampa Mendoza, who first came to the islands from Portugal to work cattle on the north end of the island, but ended up working the ocean instead.

And now Dad fished the same waters, day after sunbaked day with his sampan, usually without even a half day of rest in between. When the fish were running every boat in the harbor went out. When the fish were silent the pier was lazy with waiting fishermen.

Once I asked Dad where the fish went when they weren't biting.

"They run in schools, *thousands* of them, all over the place," he said, waving his hand out toward the horizon. "They follow the currents."

I pictured schools of monkeypod leaves shimmering in tree-top canopies, turning together in the trade winds.

"When the currents hit the islands," he went on, "they break up and swirl around the reefs. That's where the food is, in the reefs. All kinds of fish come around—marlin, *abi, mahimahi, ono, opakapaka*." Dad watched my face as I listened. Then he smiled and rubbed his hand over my head. "To know where to find them, Sonny—that's the trick."

I whispered "*opakapaka*" over and over, until I could say it as well as Dad.

I couldn't remember the first time Dad took me out in the skiff. My memories of being bundled up in the life vest went back to a point, then it all got confusing, my thoughts always turning fuzzy, shadowy. They came to me in pieces, parts of a strange puzzle. I didn't know if they were real or part of a dream I'd had a long time ago. I'd get these glimpses when I least expected it, but never enough to make any sense.

I moved to the bow with my face to the sea, piercing the air as we moved through it. Dark blotches of giant coral heads loomed in the sand below. The sides of Dad's wooden skiff hummed through my fingers under the buzz of the old, silver, ten-horse Mercury.

He was taking me to a secret cove, I thought, somewhere along the coast, a place where only the two of us existed. I hoped it would be a shallow spot, a beach with no waves.

The whine of the outboard echoed out over the empty harbor. Dad almost had to shout for me to hear him. "When I was a small boy," he said, "your grampa made me and your two uncles jump off the end of the pier. We had to swim back by ourselves. Your uncle Raz was even younger than you are. Harley could already swim pretty good, but Raz and I couldn't even dog paddle. Scared the hell out of me. But we learned to swim, all right. Or else he would have let us sink. He was pretty tough, your grampa."

I couldn't remember much of Grampa Mendoza, only that he'd once made a nickel go through my head, from one ear to the other. He didn't visit us very much. He and Tutu Mendoza had moved to the island of Oahu before I was born.

"You've got to learn how to swim as well as you know how to walk," Dad went on. He pointed out to sea with his chin. "Looks peaceful, huh?" I turned and blinked, the horizon low, and far away. "Well, it is—now," he said. "But there will be times when it will try to kill you."

When we reached the farthest mooring from the pier, Dad slowed the skiff and pointed to the buoy. I grabbed the white, beachball-sized float as Dad cut the engine.

"Far as we go, son. . . . It's time."

I stared at him, and he studied me with his earth-brown eyes.

"You ready?"

I shrugged, and Dad laughed. The ocean moved through the thin wooden hull under my bare feet as I stood facing him.

Dad removed my life vest and pulled me up next to him. Being in the skiff without the vest on sent a shiver through me. I searched for something to hang on to, but Dad's arm was pliant and smooth, and not at all secure.

"You can do it," he whispered. Then slowly, working against my tightening grip, Dad lowered me into the water.

My whole body surged with a wave of fear, my arms and legs shaking. I clawed at Dad, leaving red lines down his arms. A school of small gray fish that was gathered around the buoy turned in a simultaneous wave and rushed off. I raked the air and scratched at Dad and fumbled around the side of the skiff, but quickly gave it up to grab the float.

I took short, shallow gulps of air that made me dizzy, kicking wildly and trying to climb up on the buoy. The ocean below felt a thousand fathoms deep. I could feel it sucking at me, reaching up, pulling down, pulling down.

Dad took the oar and paddled the skiff off about twenty feet. "Swim to me," he called.

The buoy kept turning and popping out beside me. My fingers slipped and I grabbed the mossy chain that sank to the sand below. My legs searched frantically for the right moves, but my head kept sinking under. The salty ocean stung my eyes and filled my mouth.

I yelled to Dad between gulps of air and water, but he wouldn't come back for me. I caught glimpses of him sitting calmly in the skiff through my splashing and churning. He seemed so far away.

"Relax, Sonny, don't work so hard."

While he waited for me to settle down he dropped the glass-bottom box over the side and looked into it. Sharks, eels, and stingrays raced through my mind and gathered like ghosts around my legs. I pulled my feet up close to me, but had to let them down again to kick.

I let go of the buoy and tried to swim to the skiff the way I pretended to swim in the cove with Keo when I kicked the sandy bottom. Now, my foot sank, and pulled me down with it. Water raced into my mouth and gagged me.

I pulled myself back up and clawed the sea, arms and legs reaching, and finding nothing. I began to sink again, sucking for air and taking in large, painful gulps of water. I tried to scream but couldn't. My legs and arms felt like dead rubber, my hands . . . my . . .

Then I hit something solid.

The oar.

Dad had reached out so I could grab the blade. I pulled it close and climbed it hand over hand to the skiff, moving fast and deliriously. Dad reached out and pulled me aboard like a fresh-caught fish.

I sat opposite him in the bow, shivering with adrenaline, muscles sapped and shuddering, dripping, and coughing.

Don't ever do that again, boy! Never! The sudden dream-memory ran through my mind, settling nowhere. But coming from where? *Don't ever . . . Don't ever . . .*

My jaw wouldn't stop quivering.

After I caught my breath I glanced in toward the pier. Keo was standing on the hood of someone's Jeep with his hand shading his eyes, watching. I was glad he couldn't see my legs shaking and catch the fear in my eyes.

Dad sat waiting, bent forward with his elbows on his knees. "You did fine," he said. "Take a rest." He paused. "Your mother would be proud of you, Sonny. But she never would have approved. She called your grampa *barbaric* when I told her how I learned to swim. She was a good swimmer, though, better than me. And you would have learned a couple of years ago if she'd been around."

I tried not to look at Dad, wanting him to think I was still too tired to go back in the water. But he fell silent. When I peeked up and saw him staring at his hands I knew he was thinking about my mother. He had a habit of studying them whenever he thought of things that couldn't be explained, or things that refused to be put to rest.

Aunty Pearl had told me about my mother when I started asking why I lived with Keo and Uncle Harley and her, and not with my father in his house down by the ocean. She told me my mother had died just a few months after I was born. I understood that she was gone, and that I would never see her. But why couldn't I live with Dad?

"Your daddy is always out fishing," Aunty Pearl had said. "What could he do with a baby, anyway. And I loved taking care of you." She'd put her hand on my face. It was hot, but I liked it. I tried to picture Dad holding a baby, but couldn't. Aunty Pearl was probably right about that part. "Oh Sonny," she went on, "your mama was so beautiful . . . pure-blooded French, with skin as smooth as oriental silk. She made me feel like I was important to her—she'd look right into my eyes whenever we talked. We all loved her . . . But your daddy hurt the most. It's the only time I've ever seen him cry. He would have done anything for her. Anything."

Dad paddled the skiff back to the buoy, and again dropped me over the side. The ocean engulfed me, with only my head above the surface, from my chin up. This time I held the float and let my legs sink, feeling the smallest hint of confidence. I strained to find Keo on the pier, but he was gone.

I shook away thoughts of eels or sharks below me in the water, and concentrated on Dad. Again I let go of the buoy and splashed my way through the placid afternoon sea, fighting the relentless downward pull.

Dad made me swim to the skiff from the buoy over and over

and over, until I had no strength left in me. Every now and then he would yell a word of encouragement, and always, when I reached the skiff, pull me aboard and let me rest.

Each time, while he waited for my breathing to slow, he searched the ocean floor through the glass-bottom box. After what must have been my tenth trip from the buoy, he called me to take a look at the heel of an old green bottle he'd spotted sticking out of the sand on the bottom. Then he pointed out the faint thread of a trail, looking as if someone had taken their finger and traced a thin line in the sand far below.

"Sometimes when you dig around the end of those trails," he said, "you can find a shell."

Dad slipped into the water and appeared below me. He dove as effortlessly as a porpoise, as much a part of the sea as he was of the land. I tried to hold my breath as long as he did, but it was impossible.

I held the glass-bottom box as still as I could and watched as he approached the trail from behind, slowly moving his hand under the sand, like slipping it under a sheet, searching for the buried shell.

The sandy bottom around Dad suddenly exploded, turning into a cloud of undersea dust, rising upward, shooting outward. Dad struggled backward, frantically reversing himself, trying to get away. I saw a whiplike shape slash by his chest, narrowly missing him. From the growing cloud a huge, winged creature that had buried itself in the sand burst forth and shot away from where Dad floundered. It soared out, the fastest thing I'd ever seen under water. Then it circled back in a wide arc, diamond-shaped, with two hornlike arms sticking out in front, and a thin tail flowing out behind. Dad rose to the surface, the dust cloud spreading outward below him, and moving beyond the corners of the glass-bottom box.

He pulled himself into the skiff. My heart thumped in my chest like waves whomping at the seawall. He'd been *bit*!

"That one . . . got by me . . ." Dad said after he caught his breath. "Caught him . . . while he was asleep . . . Didn't even know he was there."

"What *was* it?" I asked.

Dad let his breathing slow and didn't answer right away. I searched his body for a cut, a sting, but found nothing.

"Manta ray," he finally said. "They don't bother people . . . but they can sure scare the hell out of you." Dad began adjusting the strap on his face mask, his breathing still heavy.

"I want you to come down with me," he said as if nothing had happened. He put the face mask on my head and pulled the glass down over my eyes. "Come on, let's go take a look."

I ripped the mask off and he put it back on again.

"But . . . but the *manta ray* . . ." I said.

The vision of Dad backing away from the whip stayed with me—the explosion, the flashing tail, and the plume of dust billowing outward. The image kept repeating: explosion, Dad reeling, explosion, Dad reeling. *Don't ever do that again, boy!*

"Don't worry about him," Dad said. "Rays don't bother people, they're peaceful. And besides, he's probably half a mile down the coast by now."

I pulled the mask off again and peered into the glass-bottom box one more time. The ray was gone. Dad patiently put the mask back on me and told me to breathe through my mouth. He looked fuzzy through the glass. I felt like I was peering out into a world where I didn't belong.

He dropped over the side of the skiff and held his arms up for me, barely moving, his fins sustaining him, as if he were standing on the bottom. I held on to the seat. If Keo had been there he'd have jumped in on his own, and I'd watch him from the skiff, wobbling his way down to the bottom. He wouldn't quite make it, but he'd tell me he did.

"Don't try to swim," Dad said, "just take a big breath and

hold it. Then sink down with me. Don't worry, I'll bring you back up."

The world went silent as we sank. The mask pushed in on my face and small streams of water dripped in at my temples. The ocean filled my ears and pressed in painfully. We floated in an air of watery space with a crackling, snapping, buzzing sound all around us. A small puddle began to gather in the mask, below my nose, nearly panicking me.

But for a moment I looked beyond the puddle, amazed at the islands of coral that broke the sandy ocean floor. Silent fish circled and hung in small schools far beneath my feet, their backs dark and bullet shaped. A huge parrot fish nibbled at the edge of a mass of coral, then suddenly darted away and sailed to a stop farther out.

Off toward even deeper water, where everything turned fuzzy and shadowy blue, the long, ghostly chain of the buoy sank to a grayish slab of mossy concrete.

Dad turned slowly, so that I could see all the way around. The undersea world seemed to rush at me, like a towering wave slamming the shore and racing up the sand.

With both hands I squeezed Dad's arm to get him to take us up, but froze when I saw just beyond him a foot-long, green fish, motionless, watching me with one round eye. A harmless stickfish, as close as I'd ever seen one. I kicked and grabbed at Dad, and the fish vanished, shooting off into the distance as suddenly as it had appeared.

On our way back to the pier Dad let me rest my hand on the throttle and pilot the skiff through the harbor. I was so tired that everything around me seemed dreamlike. The long red roof of Kona Inn stretched sharp and comforting within the thick, green grove of palms that lined the shore, just above a sketch of white foam.

Dad sat next to me in the stern on the other side of the engine, his arms lean and muscular, his chest hairless and a deep red-brown.

I studied the coral heads as we passed over them. It wasn't so bad, I thought. I could do it again.

I could, if I wanted to.

But I could almost feel the solid, hot concrete of the pier under my bare feet.

Dad looked long at his sampan as we eased by. Three white letters sailed across its blue transom. *Ipo*. Sweetheart. The name Dad had given my mother.

With Dad's help I made a long, slow turn around the boat, close enough to see salt dried on its hull. It rode at its mooring as easily as an old coconut floating in a tidal pool. Dad faced away from me, looking at the thirty-foot sampan he spent his life on. I peeked around him trying to see if I could see what Dad saw.

Keo was alone in the cove, floating on one of the tubes. Small waves from the skiff rocked him as we passed by. Dad let me out near shore and headed back over to the small boat landing.

Keo rolled off the tube and swam out into the cove, out to the deepest point. "Come on out," he yelled.

I stared back at him, my arms hanging at my sides like old frayed rope.

"Chicken," he shouted. "*Buk-buk-buk-bu-gock!*"

The ocean rose to my knees, my waist, then my chest, as I slowly waded in. When it reached my chin I started swimming, madly kicking and clawing at the ocean. Water exploded all around me, splashing clumsily over my face and blurring my vision. I aimed my chin to the sky and thrashed out to Keo, swimming past him, circling him, then heading back to the beach. I caught a glimpse of Dad watching from the pier.

Keo pawed at the water when he swam, too, but easily, without splashing. "Let's dive to the bottom," he said.

I didn't answer. I barely made it back to shore.

A half hour later, Dad came down and sat next to me on the sand. Keo was out in the water, hanging over the edge of one of the inner tubes, motionless, as if asleep.

"You did a good job out there today, Sonny," Dad said, pointing out to the harbor with his chin. Then, after a moment of silence, he added, "I'm proud of you."

Keo looked up and saw us, and started kicking in to shore.

Dad stood, as if shaken out of a daydream. "It's time for a couple of changes," he said. "Tell Keo to come, we're going for a ride."

Dad walked over to his Jeep while Keo came up from the water, holding the dripping black tube over his shoulder.

Dad drove up the rocky driveway to our house, dust rising behind the Jeep and spreading into the dry trees. Aunty Pearl strolled out onto the porch with her black hair pulled behind her head and curled into a tight knot. She waved down to us as we bounced into the yard, her small hand almost lost on an arm as thick as my stomach. She looked exactly like the old pictures of Hawaiian queens, wide and tall, draped in full-length muumuus, with huge bare feet as tough as coconut husks. If an orchid was beautiful, then Aunty Pearl was a thousand of them put together.

Keo's scruffy dogs, Bullet and Blossom, set off a racket of barking. Aunty Pearl shushed them by clapping her hands.

Off to the right and slightly downhill Uncle Harley's icehouse stood like a huge, windowless box, almost half the size of the main house. He made ice for boats in there, and kept fish before trucking them over to the market on the other side of the island. A small, fenced-in pigpen with shady, corrugated iron shelters flowed off the uphill side, big enough for three or four good-sized pigs.

The dogs leaped at us as we drove up to the house. Keo jumped out of the Jeep. "Come on," he said. "Let's go see the pigs."

I started running after him.

"Sonny, wait," Dad called. "Come up to the house for a minute." Keo kept on going without turning back.

Aunty Pearl gave us both a hug. It had only been a few hours since I'd seen her, but still she crushed me to her as if I'd been gone a month. She frowned at Dad. "So what are you doing up here in the middle of a perfectly good fishing day?"

Dad looked down at me and rubbed his hand over my head, then put his arm on my shoulder. "I think I can handle it now, Pearl."

Aunty Pearl put her hand to her cheek, then hugged us again, and started crying. She couldn't talk for a few minutes, because she would start crying every time she tried. Finally, she motioned us into the house.

Keo started walking back toward us kicking an old can.

Dad and I followed Aunty Pearl to the room that Keo and I shared. I thought I knew what Dad was saying, but I didn't want to think about it in case it wasn't true. Then he and Aunty Pearl started taking my clothes out of the dresser.

Keo burst into the room. "Hey, what's going on?"

Aunty Pearl put her arm around him and pulled him up close. "Sonny's going home, Keo—to live down by the beach with his father." Then she turned to me. "But you'll be back for lots of visits, won't you, Sonny?"

I nodded, but must have looked as if I weren't sure, because Aunty Pearl pulled Keo in closer, and started crying again.

Dad's old wooden house stood up on stilts, with three or four feet between the floor and the ground. "To keep rats and mongooses out," he'd told me.

Kiawe and coconut trees surrounded the long, rectangular yard and swooped up behind us to the road that ran along the coast from Kailua to Keauhou. Dad parked the Jeep on the grass, his five dogs whining and wagging their tails as we pulled up to the house.

"You can have my room," Dad said as we walked in. It was the only bedroom. Dad nodded toward the big couch in the front room, the place I always slept when I came to stay for a day or two. "I like to sleep out here, anyway," he said.

Except for the few things I'd brought with me, nothing in the place was mine. But there was nothing I owned, or could think of owning, that I wouldn't have given up to be right there with Dad. Now, and forever, only one thin wall would stand between his bed and mine.

"Before we unpack your things," Dad said, dropping the cardboard box of clothes on the kitchen table, "let's go down to the ocean, maybe take a quick swim. It's hotter than a dump fire around here." I'd had enough swimming that day, but I didn't mind.

I followed him down the porch stairs and out across the grass to the water. You could look out and see the horizon, miles and miles away, with only the clean, blue and turquoise expanse of ocean between the yard and the end of the world. Dad's dogs followed, then trotted out ahead, sniffing everything in sight as if they'd never been there before.

The shoreline was mostly lava, with a few good-sized sandy patches nestled around small tidal pools. Dad and I picked our way out over the rocks to the water, which sparkled under the late afternoon sky. Small waves hissed in and surrounded us as we eased into the ocean, Dad leading the way, and me trailing behind, turning the water white as I churned through it.

I suddenly realized that I was *swimming*—out over my

head, in deep water. I tried to keep up with Dad, but got tired and had to go back to shore.

The powdery sand patches were hot and comforting. I sat down in one and stared back out at Dad, now making long, quiet dives to the bottom. Sudden sleep tugged at my eyes, and I fell back on one elbow, then lay down completely, the low sun quickly turning the water on my face to fine salt crystals. Warmth curled around my shoulders from the sand stuck to my back and arms.

The last thing I remembered before Dad woke me was thinking of the earth as a woman. Someone like Aunty Pearl, surrounding me with strong arms, and rocking me to sleep with soft humming.

"Don't run out of gas yet, Sonny," Dad said. "We still have a big *mahimahi* to eat. I think you can handle half of it—at least from what I can tell by what I've seen today." He was bent over me, water streaming off his deep-tanned shoulders. He pulled me up and brushed some of the sand off my back.

When Dad started back up to the house, the dogs spread out ahead, sweeping over the rocks.

Stepping where Dad stepped, I followed him home.

2

Malanamekahuluohemanu

(1956)

Uncle Raz stood at the edge of Uncle Harley's pigpen with his arms draped over the fence. The sun looked white in the humid air, and the island was as still as the inside of a car with the windows up. "I bet Pearl weighs more than the pig," Uncle Raz said.

Dad, Keo, and I glanced over at Uncle Harley, standing there next to Uncle Raz, staring down at the pig as if he hadn't heard. We waited, almost without breathing. He'd never let Uncle Raz get away with a remark like that.

Uncle Raz puckered up his face. "That damn thing smells worse than a pile of rotten fish, Harley. I don't know how you can keep it around your house."

Dad and I had driven up to help Uncle Harley figure out what to do about slaughtering the pig. Keo was nine, and I was eight, and, like Uncle Harley, we'd grown to love old Alii, like we loved the dogs, even though we knew long ago that the day would come when the pig would be butchered.

Uncle Harley snapped his fingers twice. "Alii, come here, boy."

The pig came lumbering over and Uncle Harley reached down and scratched him behind his ears. Looking at the hairy, blunt, mud-caked nose, and small half-open eyes, anyone could see how easy it would be to get attached to him. He was a Hawaiian pig, a boar with his tusks cut off, and had long, black, bristly hair that felt like nylon fishing leader. He looked pretty mean, and if you didn't know him you wouldn't get anywhere near the fence. But Uncle Harley had captured him young and he was as calm and as tame as old Blossom.

"Must weigh a ton," Uncle Raz said. "Probably have to clean it right here in the pigpen."

Uncle Harley kept his hand on Alii's head. "Probably about three-sixty, three-seventy is all. What do you think, Raymond?"

"Big enough," Dad said. "It's going to take all three of us to carry the bugger after we shoot him."

No one spoke for a few minutes after that. It was the pig's last day.

Uncle Raz, as usual, broke the silence and moved our thoughts into easier territory. "So what, Harley, you want to put twenty bucks on who weighs more? The pig, or Pearl?"

"Sheese!" Dad stepped away and shook his head.

"No, really," Uncle Raz said. "How much does Pearl weigh?" Was he *serious*?

Uncle Harley just stared down at the pig. Then he pushed himself back from the fence and said, "I've never asked her how much she weighs. Maybe she doesn't even know herself."

"Well, I think Pearl weighs more," Uncle Raz said.

"No, the pig weighs more."

"Twenty bucks," Uncle Raz said.

Uncle Harley smiled at him. It could have been me and Keo

smiling like that, after me telling Keo there was no way he could ride Alii for more than five seconds. If there was anything that kept our family together it was a challenge.

Uncle Harley put his arm on Keo's shoulder and pulled him up against his side. "Okay, hotshot," he said to Uncle Raz. "Put a hundred down and you got a bet."

Dad snickered. That would shut Uncle Raz up pretty quick. Keo shifted his eyes in my direction. We'd never heard Uncle Harley go over thirty dollars before. A hundred sounded like betting a Jeep or a boat.

Uncle Raz's eyes darted around like he was adding it up. He stuck out his hand. "Easy money, sucker."

Their knuckles turned white when they shook.

"If Maxine finds out about this, you'd both be better off as shark bait," Dad said. "She'll probably smell this one a mile away." He was referring to Aunty Pearl's mother, Tutu Max. "And there's another problem," Dad went on. "Easy to weigh the pig, but what about Pearl?"

The three of them thought for a moment with puzzled faces, Dad standing between his two brothers, an inch or so taller than both of them. Uncle Raz was the shortest, and the youngest, with a slight bulge in his stomach from too much beer. Dad was thin, but muscular, and darker from being out on his boat. Uncle Harley was muscular, too, but not in the sharp, chiseled way Dad was. He was the oldest, and also the softest. He was always cuddling up to Aunty Pearl. The two of them fit together like a tug and a barge.

Uncle Raz stood barefoot in the powdery dirt with his hands in his pockets, jingling change. "Shoot him today, or what?" He sure had a way of getting under your skin sometimes.

"Nope. Tomorrow's soon enough," Uncle Harley said in a low voice.

"Hey, don't get pantie," Uncle Raz said. "Let's go have a beer and figure this out. It's gonna take some thinking to get Pearl on a scale."

"Hah," Uncle Harley said. "If you knew what you're getting yourself into you'd just pay me and forget the whole thing." Uncle Harley glanced over at Dad and flicked his eyebrows. Something passed between them that I couldn't translate. "We can do it, though."

Keo didn't seem to be bothered at all, even though Aunty Pearl was his mother.

"Keo," Uncle Harley said. "Go get three beers."

Keo took off up to the house and I followed. "A *hundred dollars*," I said as we ran.

"Dad would never bet a hundred dollars unless he knew he could win," Keo said. "I don't know *how*, but he'll win all right."

Inside the house Aunty Pearl was sitting at the kitchen table peeling potatoes. She was humming "Akaka Falls," her voice so soothing it made me stop and listen. Her gold wedding ring was almost lost in the puffy skin that bunched up around it. She'd probably never be able to take it off, even if she wanted to. Though she never mentioned it, I always thought she had royal blood in her. The bigger the Hawaiian queens were, the more beautiful. Keo was lucky that way, because he had the blood, too.

Aunty Pearl smiled at us and pointed toward a wooden bowl full of red-orange mangoes.

"Thanks, Aunty." I reached for a fat one.

"Dad wants some beer," Keo said, already opening the icebox.

"So early? It's not even lunchtime yet. What are those Mendoza boys up to out there anyway?"

"The pig. Dad doesn't want to kill it."

"Ahhh," Aunty Pearl said in a long outward breath. "That's

what I told him when he brought it home. 'What you going do with that thing?' I said. 'Feed him, get him fat, maybe sell him, or have a luau,' your daddy said. 'You think you can give him up after you raise him,' I said, 'or worse, shoot him and eat him? You crazy, Harley.' Your daddy's too soft, Keo. He's too good inside to do that. But I guess he has to find out for himself."

Aunty Pearl thought for a moment. "That Raz and your fathers are just a bunch of boys who don't want to grow up. But that's all right, they're good boys. And I like Daddy just the way he is. If he grew up he'd just get cranky."

Keo put three cold beers on the table and picked out a mango for himself. A chicken clucked outside the open kitchen window. Sweat came out of Aunty Pearl's hair and trailed down her temples. "Sonny," she said. "Put some food in the tank, just a couple of pinches."

Aunty Pearl's thirty-gallon aquarium sat on the counter behind me, the pump vibrating through the glass sides. Uncle Harley had built it for her when it became too hard for Aunty Pearl to go down to the pier every day like she and Uncle Harley had done for years. As time had passed, she'd gotten bigger and bigger, and moving around had almost become too much for her. Now she mostly stayed home with her goldfish and swordtails, instead of watching the boats come in.

Keo stuck a bottle of beer in the back pocket of his shorts and grabbed the other two in one hand. We walked out of the kitchen leaving Aunty Pearl shaking her head. "Don't worry, boys," she called after us. "I know that man. He's soft."

Outside, Dad and his two brothers were leaning up against the Jeep and Uncle Raz's shiny red Toyota pickup. Uncle Raz was laughing at something Uncle Harley had said. "This I gotta see," he said. "This I gotta see."

I glanced at Keo. He shrugged his shoulders.

Dad said, "I always thought you were a little off, Harley. Making ice, selling fish, and raising a pig doesn't give your brain any exercise. Maybe you better take up something that makes you sweat a little."

Keo handed them the beer. We hung around hoping they'd give us a clue as to what was going on.

"Tonight," Uncle Harley said.

A fly buzzed near my ear and I brushed it away.

Dad, Uncle Raz, and I drove back up later, squeezed together in the front seat of the Toyota. Uncle Harley and Aunty Pearl were sitting on the porch watching the sunset and Keo was in the yard shooting at a saki bottle with his BB gun. Bullet and Blossom came barking up to us.

We were all dressed for the occasion in shorts and clean T-shirts, and acting as innocent as Aunty Pearl herself.

Three empty beer bottles stood in a neat row on the side of Uncle Harley's wooden chair. He'd put on a blue aloha shirt and had slicked back his hair.

Aunty Pearl was dressed in a nice muumuu—red, with yellow and white flowers. Her hand surrounded Uncle Harley's. He always looked smaller when he sat with her on the porch.

"You ready?" Dad called.

"Ready as ever," Uncle Harley answered with a grin.

Aunty Pearl seemed pretty happy, but it was hard to tell for sure because the pinched fleshiness of her face gave her a kind of permanent look that was difficult to read.

I went up on the porch and gave her a hug. I did that every time I came up, even if I was just there a few hours before. Small beads of perspiration dotted her upper lip, but the heat of the day had passed and it was beginning to cool down some. No matter how hot it was, she always seemed happy to see me.

Keo and I followed Dad, Uncle Harley, and Uncle Raz to the pigpen. "Want to double it?" Uncle Harley asked, looking Uncle Raz straight in the eye. "Two hundred bucks?"

Dad looked at Uncle Harley like he'd just made a huge

blunder. Uncle Raz's jaw dropped slightly. He glanced over at Dad, then back at Uncle Harley. Then he smirked. "You're on, sucker of suckers."

Uncle Harley seemed happier than usual, as if he knew something that no one else knew. But then he always looked that way when a bet was at stake. He swung his arm out in the direction of Uncle Raz's Toyota. "Bring your truck to the ramp."

The ramp was something Uncle Harley had cooked up for Aunty Pearl so she wouldn't be stuck at home so much. Uncle Harley no longer had the strength to lift her into the front seat of his truck, even if she could have fit, which we all began to doubt. So he built a small rock retaining wall and spent a couple of days dumping dirt behind it, shaping it and tapping it into a long, easy ramp. It worked perfectly.

"Keo, Sonny," Uncle Harley called. "Go get Alii."

Keo went into the pigpen and tied a rope around Alii's neck. Then, dangling a fishtail in front of him, we coaxed him out to the ramp. It was a good thing Keo had thought about the rope because Alii got a little nervous when Bullet and Blossom whisked around him yipping and yapping.

"You boys ride with the pig," Uncle Harley said after we got Alii into the back of Uncle Raz's truck. "Keep him from moving around when we get out on the road."

"Where are we taking him?" Keo asked.

"You'll see." It was clear that Uncle Harley didn't want us asking any questions.

Uncle Raz moved the truck away from the ramp and Dad backed Uncle Harley's truck into its place. Uncle Harley went up to the porch to help Aunty Pearl. She looked happy. She loved going places.

Dad dropped the tailgate on the truck and waited while Uncle Harley ceremoniously accompanied Aunty Pearl from the house, down the dirt yard, and up the ramp. Aunty Pearl walked onto the bed of the pickup and sat gracefully down on a special upholstered seat that ran from side to side just behind the cab. She looked up at Uncle Harley and smiled, then raised her hand. Uncle Harley squeezed it.

The bed of the truck had sunk at least two inches when she stepped onto it. She was *some* woman. Her Hawaiian name was Malanamekahuluohemanu, light as the feather of a bird. A name that fit her spirit perfectly.

"Okay, let's go," Uncle Harley said, climbing into the cab. But we didn't get two feet before Grampa Joe and Tutu Max came roaring up the dirt driveway in their rusting Impala, a cloud of dust billowing out behind them.

If anyone could mess up a nice plan, Tutu Max could.

Tutu Max was driving, as usual. Next to her, Grampa Joe looked like a pet dog leaning against the door with his nose out the window. They pulled up next to Uncle Harley's truck. Tutu Max looked over at her daughter.

"Hoo-ie, Pearl honey, where you off to?" Tutu Max asked, ignoring Uncle Harley.

Aunty Pearl smiled down at her. "Downtown. The pier. See the boats and fish."

Like a wary cat trying to keep watch over her trusting, openhearted kitten, Tutu Max had a habit of always checking up on her child, even though Aunty Pearl had been married to Uncle Harley for more than ten years.

"Why the pig over there?" Tutu Max asked, hooking her thumb over toward Keo and me.

"Gonna weigh him. Tomorrow Daddy going shoot 'um," she said in the smooth, lilting, Hawaiian-style English she and Tutu Max spoke.

Tutu Max looked sideways over at Uncle Harley. He nodded slowly and lifted his wrist from the steering wheel in a lazy wave, holding his hand open, fingers spread, like signaling the number five.

Tutu Max squinted her eyes. "Why's the pig in the truck?"

"Like the last supper," Uncle Harley said. "You know, like when they plan to shoot a prisoner the next day they give him what he wants for dinner? Same thing. Only this is a last ride." He smiled after he said it, knowing he'd given her a good answer without having given her an answer at all. Uncle Harley once told Keo and me that Tutu Max was the nosiest person he'd ever known.

Tutu Max glared at Uncle Harley. She knew he was a master at the straight-face lie. And ever since Aunty Pearl broke her foot climbing onto Uncle Raz's boat, Tutu Max had become as protective of her as a starving cat with a fish head. The fact that Uncle Harley mostly ignored her and usually just went about whatever he was doing didn't help.

Tutu Max turned back to Aunty Pearl. "How long you going be gone?" she asked.

"Couple hours."

"We wait here for you," Tutu Max said.

Grampa Joe had yet to say a word. But no one expected him to, not when Tutu Max was around.

"Fresh *sashimi* in the icebox," Aunty Pearl said. "We come back soon."

Keo and I waved as we pulled away. The pig got a little jumpy and we had to hold on to him.

I looked forward, to the back of Uncle Harley's truck. Long, loose strands of hair flew across Aunty Pearl's face. She nearly filled the seat from one side of the truck to the other. Once when we were out fishing, Uncle Harley told me that Aunty Pearl was the kindest and most beautiful woman he'd ever known. There was nothing she owned, he said, that she wouldn't give to someone else who needed it. And if something was bothering you, she'd come over and sit by you, and talk about all kinds of things that had nothing to do with your problem. But pretty soon you'd be pouring your heart out.

She had a way, he said. He didn't know what he'd done in his life to deserve it, but he was the luckiest man on the Big Island.

The torches along the water at Kona Inn had already been lit by the time we got to the pier, and the sky was a golden-orange from the sun just disappearing below the horizon. The serene, wavering sigh of a Hawaiian steel guitar, wrapped within the sweet smell of cooking steak, drifted out from the restaurants and gave me a warm, comfortable feeling, as if all I could ever want out of life was already around me.

We parked on the pier with the front of the truck facing away from the bay so Aunty Pearl could sit and watch the charter boats come in. She was a sight, sitting there surrounded by Uncle Harley and a good-sized collection of her countless friends and relatives. Some sat in the bed of the truck with her, like servants at the feet of the queen. People who'd never seen Aunty Pearl before watched from a distance, amazed. Aunty Pearl smiled at everyone, and waved.

The *Kakina* was just in and its crew was hoisting a fat blue marlin from the water. As the fish rose to the pier, a watery stream of blood and ocean flowed into the harbor from its rough bill. A man pulled the hoist around and swung the fish in over the pier. The skipper called out the weight. "Eight hundred forty-two pounds." A murmur rose from the crowd.

Uncle Harley, Dad, Uncle Raz, and a couple of their friends stood around Aunty Pearl drinking beer and passing stories around. By seven-thirty almost everyone had gone home.

With Alii snoring in the truck, Keo and I squatted on our heels at the edge of the pier, staring into the darkening harbor and watching reflections of town lights shimmy out across the water. Keo had been pretty quiet all afternoon, mostly just taking in what was going on and keeping an eye on Aunty Pearl.

"Raz, back your truck up to the scale," Uncle Harley said, startling me. "Keo, Sonny, get in the back with the pig."

"What you going do, Daddy?" Aunty Pearl asked.

"Weigh the pig," Uncle Harley said.

"Oh, good idea."

Dad rigged a sling out of an old torn tarp and wrapped it around Alii's belly. He tied it tight with wire fishing leader and looped the wire over the hook on the fish hoist. Uncle Raz pulled on the chain and Alii rose from the bed of the truck. Keo and I held him steady and kept him from getting too excited. His grunts and screeches were deep and rich, coming from way down inside him.

When he was three or four inches off the bed of the truck, Uncle Harley called for Dad to read the scale.

"Three sixty," he called. "No, wait, three sixty-two."

"Not bad, not bad," Uncle Raz said, unimpressed.

"Yeah," Uncle Harley said, ignoring the flatness in Uncle Raz's voice. "Hard to beat that." He looked at Uncle Raz with a face that invited him to add another couple of bucks to the bet.

Uncle Raz ignored him. "Hard, but not impossible," he said.

"What's the weight?" Aunty Pearl called from the truck, which was parked far enough away that she couldn't hear what Uncle Harley and Uncle Raz were saying.

Dad called over to Aunty Pearl, "Three sixty-two."

"Hooo-ie!" she said.

"Okay, now what," asked Uncle Raz, in a low, mumbling voice.

Uncle Harley turned his back to Aunty Pearl. "Don't worry," he said. Then he called to Dad to get some more beer.

I went with him, following him down to Taneguchi's market. We walked slowly, the pavement of the pier warm under my bare feet. How would Dad feel if he were in Uncle Harley's shoes, if Aunty Pearl were *my* mother? Would *be* make a bet about her? Dad hardly ever talked about my mother, and I was starting to wonder why.

"Dad," I said, just before we reached the store, "what do you think about Uncle Harley and Uncle Raz making a bet about Aunty Pearl?"

At first he just kept on walking. When we went into the bright lights of the market, he said, "None of my business what Harley does, but I'll tell you this: he wouldn't do anything to hurt Pearl."

Dad pulled two six-packs of Oly out of the cooler and headed to the cash register as if everything in life was as it should be.

When we returned with the beer, Uncle Harley walked over to us. "If we're not home soon, nosy Max is going to come poking around." He looked down the road that ran along the seawall.

Uncle Raz came over for the beer. "She's had eight beers already. Pretty soon she's going to want to get out of the truck."

Keo and I were beginning to figure the whole thing out. Aunty Pearl hardly ever got out of the truck when we went to the pier. But when she had too many beers she became extremely happy and would do unexpected things. We found that out one night when we'd all gone to a big luau down at Kahaluu beach. Aunty Pearl gave us each a beer, which she'd never have done in her right mind.

The plan was simple. Get Aunty Pearl full of beer, step number one. Then for sure she'd want to get out of the truck to take a long, slow walk on the pier with Uncle Harley. She loved to do that. The key to the whole thing was in her wanting to get out of the truck. There was really only one way to do it: the fish hoist. And while Uncle Harley was lifting her from the truck, someone would just happen to look up at the scale.

Keo climbed into the truck and sat near his mother. I glared at Uncle Harley whenever I got the chance to catch his eye.

By eight o'clock Aunty Pearl had downed three more beers and was starting to laugh at anything anyone said. Uncle Harley squeezed onto the seat next to her with one leg hanging over the side of the truck. He told jokes and wild stories, his arm around Aunty Pearl's neck. With his free hand he gave her beer from a cooler that he'd brought from the house. Dad and Uncle Raz shared the new six-packs.

Aunty Pearl seemed to roll in one continuous laugh. I was beginning to think that Uncle Harley had forgotten all about his plan.

Then he dropped down to the pier and stretched and called Keo and me over to him. "Run down to the end of the pier and see if Tutu Max is anywhere in sight," Uncle Harley whispered.

It was almost too dark to tell, but Keo was pretty sure that no one was coming. Just as we started back to the truck, I saw Tutu Max's car moving slowly past Emma's Store. I followed Keo and didn't tell anyone.

Aunty Pearl was standing in the truck.

"Come on, Mama," Uncle Harley said, "it's a nice night for a walk on the pier."

The color from the sunset had slipped away. The sky was black. Only two lamps cast yellow cones of light to the concrete, one above the fish scale.

Uncle Harley handed her another beer from the cooler and she guzzled it down in one take, as if it were guava juice. Dad turned away, shaking his head. I think he never stopped being amazed by his brothers. Aunty Pearl told me Dad was always the quiet one, the Mendoza boy who always did everything right. When Uncle Raz and Uncle Harley were boys, she said, they were fighting with each other all the time. But Dad was the nice one. He never got anyone's feathers up. That's why the most beautiful girl in the islands married him, she said. "She loved him so much, Sonny. And I never heard your daddy say an unkind word to her." It always made Aunty Pearl cry when she thought of my mother. "She was one of my *best* friends," she'd often tell me. And though some people made a big deal out of what race you were, Aunty Pearl had never cared that my mother was Caucasian, a *haole*. Aunty Pearl had a gentleness, something that came up and hugged you.

"Okay, Daddy, okay. How you going get me down?" Aunty Pearl said.

"Raymond, bring the chain," Uncle Harley called to Dad. "Raz, make the crossbar."

Uncle Raz pushed and slapped at Alii, who was lying on the crowbar in the truck. Alii snorted back at him, and dragged himself up. Uncle Raz wove a loop with a short length of rope and tied it to the crowbar at its midpoint. He then threw the loop over the giant hook at the end of the chain hanging from the fish scale. Dad pulled the hoist and raised the crowbar until it was even with the bed of the truck. Uncle Harley laid it at Aunty Pearl's feet.

"Okay, Mama. Stand on the bar, one foot on either side and hold tight to the chain. We'll lift you out."

Aunty Pearl moved her huge feet into position, giggling. Uncle Harley kissed her on her forehead. "You ready, Mama?"

I glanced down toward the seawall. Tutu Max and Grampa Joe had just turned onto the pier and were driving toward us with one headlight busted and the other one aimed up into the trees. "Uncle," I said. "We got company."

Uncle Harley groaned. Aunty Pearl looked off toward the one-eyed car.

Tutu Max pulled up alongside the truck and got out. "Why you still down here? What's going on? What you doing, Pearl?"

"Just getting out of the truck," Uncle Harley said quickly, all innocent.

Uncle Raz tried to keep from laughing.

"What you laughing at?" Tutu Max demanded, staring at

Uncle Raz. She was a good foot shorter than him, but a lot heavier. She took to him almost as poorly as she took to Uncle Harley. There's got to be something wrong, she said a thousand times to Uncle Raz, with a twenty-eight-year-old man who still has no wife.

Uncle Raz sobered up some and took a step backward to put some distance between himself and Tutu Max. She wasn't against using her hands to emphasize a point.

"Nothing, nothing," he said, spreading out his arms.

Tutu Max pushed by, giving Uncle Raz a shove as she passed. He fell backward, and then disappeared. I heard a plopping sound and ran to the edge of the pier. Uncle Raz popped up and reached for the truck tires that were lashed alongside the pier. Dad laughed and reached a hand down to help him.

Uncle Harley held his serious look through the whole thing.

"What's going on here, Pearl honey?" Tutu Max asked.

"Nothing, Mama. I just coming down to walk on the pier with Daddy."

"You know you have to take it easy, baby. You have to watch . . ."

"S'okay, Mama. I just coming down to walk."

Uncle Raz pulled himself up onto the pier and squatted down to squeeze the water from his clothes.

Uncle Harley said, "Okay, Mama. Hold tight and we'll bring you down."

"Wait a minute," demanded Tutu Max. "What's she standing on? Let me see. What if it breaks?"

Uncle Harley bent down and pulled the crowbar from under Aunty Pearl's feet.

"I want to try it first, from down here," Tutu Max said.

A very slight glance from Uncle Harley to his brothers laid out the whole turn of events. Dad lowered the chain. Uncle Raz stationed himself where he could take a peek at the scale. Uncle

Harley placed the crowbar on the concrete and Tutu Max stepped onto it. Dad raised her a few inches off the ground. Uncle Raz glanced at the scale and lifted an eyebrow, but kept a straight face.

Tutu Max scowled at Uncle Harley. "Okay," she said. Dad lowered her back to the pier. All this time Grampa Joe sat in the car with his door open.

With everyone offering assistance, we lowered Aunty Pearl to the pier, slowly, like the empress that she was.

It was about ten-thirty by the time we finally got her back home. Tutu Max went off with Grampa Joe to their place up the hill. Alii lumbered off the truck and headed straight for his mud hole.

Uncle Harley backed his truck up to the ramp, then climbed into the back and took Aunty Pearl's hand. She stood and smiled down at Keo and me. I half-smiled back, then stared at the ground.

Aunty Pearl started chuckling in the warm glow of the lone yard light.

"Boys," she said, and I looked back up at her. "Come to the house for a minute."

I followed Keo, both of us walking slowly behind Uncle Harley and Aunty Pearl. Uncle Harley left us on the porch.

Aunty Pearl lowered herself onto her porch chair. "Boys," she said, then paused to catch her breath. She laughed. "Boys, you look so sad." She giggled again. "Go look in the cooler in the truck. Have a beer from it," she said, then shooed us away with her hands.

Dad, Uncle Harley, and Uncle Raz stood along the fence, looking into Alii's pen. Keo and I stopped at Uncle Harley's truck and peeked into the cooler. Keo popped open a bottle with his thumb, the cap on loosely.

Water. Every beer bottle in the cooler was filled with water. She *knew*—the whole time.

Uncle Harley was a lifetime smarter than Uncle Raz, and me, for that matter.

Dad motioned for me to come over next to him. Then we all turned to Uncle Raz, waiting: *what did she weigh?*

Uncle Raz scratched his chin, then rubbed the back of his neck, then looked down and kicked at the dirt. Sometimes he drove me *crazy*.

Finally, he said, "Maxine was two sixty-eight." Then, in a low voice, added, "Pearl made three forty-seven."

"Hah!" Uncle Harley said, slapping the fence. I wanted to go stand right up next to him, I felt so good. But I just stood there.

Uncle Raz rested on the fence, his arms on the top rail, staring into the pigpen.

"S'okay, Raz," Uncle Harley said. "You can pay me tomorrow." He tapped Dad's back and winked at me.

Uncle Raz just kept on staring.

Alii snorted, then let out a long wheeze like a sigh.

Dad pushed himself away from the fence and started back to the truck. Uncle Raz and I followed.

A silky, clean offshore breeze rustled through the trees around the pigpen, and the metallic smell of nighttime coolness rose from the soil, and from the grass in the pastures. It had suddenly grown very quiet as islands at night seem to do. The three of us climbed into the front of Uncle Raz's Toyota and inched away in first gear, silent as fish.

I turned and looked back. Keo was crouching beside his father at the pigpen fence. Uncle Harley reached down and scratched Alii's ears, just like he scratched old Bullet's.

Aunty Pearl was right about the Mendoza boys. If they grew up, they'd just get cranky.

3
The Old Man
(1957)

Keo and I sat on the end of the pier on an old truck tire watching two huge sharks swim backward. When they got out about fifty or sixty feet they stopped dead in the water and stayed there, like two gray torpedoes frozen in place just under the surface of the ocean.

"Looks funny, yeah?" Keo said.

I shook my head. It was one of the strangest-looking things I'd ever seen.

The old man in the open fifteen-foot fishing skiff just off the end of the pier sat down again and waited for the sharks to return. He took off his hat and wiped the sweat from his face on the sleeve of his torn khaki shirt.

"You think he's ever seen a real shark?" Keo asked.

"I don't know," I said.

Out in the skiff the old man fanned his face with his hat.

"Looks fake," Keo said. "If that was a real shark he'd be a lot more worked up about it than *that*."

"Yeah."

"They should use real sharks, not those fake ones. Look." He pointed to the underwater cables running from the two motionless sharks to the pier. "Everyone's gonna know those are fake."

The crowd behind us was pretty quiet, mostly because there was a man who kept telling everyone to please be quiet. Someone yelled out to the man in the boat. "Ready, Mr. Tracy?"

The old man raised his hand without looking up. He looked tired.

"Action!" the man on the pier shouted. The two sharks came to life and moved in along the cables to the skiff. The old man saw them coming and stood up. "Ay! *Galanos*. Come on, *galanos*!" he shouted.

The sharks closed in on the huge, half-eaten marlin tied to the port side of the skiff. It was one of three fake marlins that were kept in a fenced-in area on the pier. One was a complete marlin, and almost looked real. Another looked about one-third eaten away. The third one was about three-quarters eaten away.

The old man struck down on the sharks with the oar, hitting them hard, but not too hard because there was a man inside each of them, in scuba gear. When he beat down into the water with the oar it reminded me of Dad at work in a shower of exploding froth, pulling in a two-hundred-pound tuna on his handline and whacking the life out of it with a baseball bat.

"Looks too fake," Keo said. He almost sounded sad.

Keo was a lot like Uncle Raz, pretty relaxed about things, but at the same time concerned about details, even if they weren't very important. Something in him just seemed to grab on and start chewing.

"A real shark," he went on, "would come up from *under* the fish and turn over to bite it. These just bump into it like canoes."

"Cut!" the man in charge called. The people behind us

clapped. The old man waved them off and sat back down in the skiff to fan his face again.

"We need to show him what a real shark looks like," Keo said.

I watched the fake ones swim back out to their spot. The water was so clear I could see the bottom. It was hot and I felt like jumping in.

"Where could *we* get a shark to show him?"

"Uncle Raz could help us," Keo said. "He knows everything there is to know about sharks."

"Don't you think he's already got too much to do, now that he's important?"

"All he has to do is show us the best place to find one."

True, I thought. But the *Optimystic*, Uncle Raz's boat, had been hired by the movie people to take the film crew back and forth to the barge they had anchored a couple of miles out to sea. He was making sixty-eight dollars a day, so we pretty much left him alone until after dark.

The old man stood against the attacking fake sharks eight more times before he came back in to the pier.

That night Keo stayed over at my house so we could concentrate on how to catch a shark for the old man. Uncle Harley and Uncle Raz both came over for a while.

Keo and I went out to the rocks and sat as close to the ocean as we could without getting hit by the small rolling swells that passed for waves in a calm sea. Dad's dogs chased black crabs into the water, and once in a while came over to stand next to us, keeping their eyes out for crabs, but wanting to be a part of what we were doing too.

"We need some horse meat," Keo said, scratching a dog's ear.

"Not easy," I said. "Who do we know that has horse meat?"

"I don't know, but I bet Grampa Joe does."

When we went back to the house, Dad, Uncle Harley, and

Uncle Raz were sitting outside on the wooden steps drinking beer. It was a peaceful sight, the three of them under the last rich stroke of orange sky slipping down off the island.

"Sixty box lunches," Uncle Raz was saying. "I take sixty box lunches out there every day. Sheese! Somebody's making some money at two fifty a box. And they got fifty-five hotel rooms!" Dad shook his head. It was pretty amazing all right.

"You going after a shark?" Uncle Harley asked.

"Ain't got time," Uncle Raz said. "Too busy."

Keo and I perked up. "What sharks?" I said.

Uncle Raz took a long swig of beer and winked at me. "Sonny's going after 'em," he said, then laughed. Dad and Uncle Harley joined him. "Mr. Sturges wants sharks. Big ones. A hundred bucks if you can catch 'em and keep 'em alive."

"Who's Mr. Sturges?" Keo asked.

"The boss of the movies."

Dad and Uncle Harley laughed again. Keo and I left. We had other things on our minds.

We decided that if we could get Grampa Joe to get us the horse meat, we'd fish for sharks down by Keahole point, where the ocean drops deep just off shore. The hundred-dollar reward, we figured, would draw attention to us, which meant we could get the old man's attention. Then we could take him to see our shark and he'd know how to poke at the fake ones on the cables and make it look real. Keo was sure of it.

Luck was with us when we called Grampa Joe the next morning and told him our plan. Tutu Max had gone to Honolulu for the week. He was as talkative as I'd ever heard him, and happy, like someone who'd just caught a big *abi*. "You boys give me two hours," he said. Grampa Joe would do anything for Keo, his only grandson. And Keo was named after him, too, which made Keo as important as King Kalakaua in Grampa Joe's eyes.

Grampa Joe got the meat and drove it down to the pier by three o'clock. He was all right, Grampa Joe. He even whispered when he told us the horse meat was in the trunk, like he was glad to be in on our secret plan. "A half a side of horse," he said. But actually it was more the size of a life preserver.

Dad, as usual, was out on his sampan, fishing for tuna. I swam out to his mooring and brought his skiff back in. We didn't have much time because I'd have to get it back before six.

Grampa Joe carried the horse meat to the skiff. It was wrapped in newspaper and burlap and smelled pretty bad. "You boys aren't the only ones fishing with horse meat today," he said. "Augie told me they had to shoot two old plugs for shark bait. I didn't tell him who I was getting it for. Don't come back till you get one, eh?"

He turned and started to walk away, kind of grufflike. But that was just his way.

"Wait!" he called. "I forgot." From the front seat of the car he pulled a white plastic five-gallon bucket with a top on it and brought it over to us. "Chum," he said, lifting the lid. "Horse guts. Bring sharks like flies to shit."

Keo took it into the skiff and Grampa Joe drove off. I kicked the engine over and took us out along the coast, north toward Keahoulu.

It took a half hour to get out to the point. We anchored in a small cove.

Because sharks like to feed at night we decided to rig a set line and leave it until morning. If we could hook one, our plan was to tow it back to the harbor, slowly, to keep it alive. Keo and I had spent hours gathering all the parts we needed for the trap. Now all we had to do was set it.

I used an eight-inch hook made of hardened steel and

connected it to about twenty feet of quarter-inch steel cable. Keo prepared the anchor and float. He dove to the bottom and wedged the clawlike anchor into a volcanic crevice so that it could endure the tug of a hooked shark. He then ran a nylon cord from the anchor to an orange float. I attached the bait line to the float line. Keo climbed back into the skiff.

The horse meat was wet and ripening. I set the hook into it firmly, yet allowing the barb freedom to do its job.

Keo opened the plastic bucket. "Yuck!"

The swirl of swishy intestines smelled like a three-day-old toad carcass. Perfect.

"It's really too early," I said. "We should be dumping this after dark."

Keo agreed, but we had no choice. We had to chum then and hope that the murky mass attracted something. Keo dropped the guts overboard in pieces, and then dumped the red liquid in after it. The water turned brown. I threw the horse meat into the middle of it. The float bobbed, sank, and reappeared.

We came back the next day just before noon. The float was gone. We circled around the cove, searching for it, saying nothing. A hooked shark could easily be tugging at the line, keeping the float beneath the surface. Or the anchor could have given way. Or the shark could have *eaten* the float.

"There!" Keo called. He pointed down into the water off the starboard bow. A tiny orange shape wobbled through the blue, far below the skiff. I shut down the engine. The quiet left behind was huge, and my ears swelled to greet it.

"Dang it . . ." I said, thinking aloud. "One of us is going to have to go down for it."

We looked at each other and laughed. It was a situation, all right. Who in his right mind wanted to jump in and see what was down there? For all we knew there was a fifteen-foot tiger shark on the hook. And neither of us had thought to bring along a pair of fins or a face mask.

"Pull out your money," Keo said. We solved all our dilemmas with coins. We each took three coins from our pockets and held them in our palms behind our backs. If I lost I'd have no choice. I shuffled two coins into one hand and kept one in the other. Keo reached out, fist tightly closed. I reached with the hand holding two coins.

"Six," he said.

"Four," I countered.

We both opened our hands and counted the coins. There were five. Keo smiled and looked me straight in the eye. We put our hands back and reshuffled the coins, each staring the other down. It wouldn't have bothered Keo in the least to dive down and take a look around. But it bothered me plenty, and Keo knew it.

On the fourth try Keo won. He didn't take his eyes off me, didn't smile. I blinked, and moved to the side of the skiff. *You're not a baby anymore.* Where did *that* come from? Another dream-memory, a mind shadow. Looking down into the water below the skiff made my stomach turn. I could almost feel the ocean gagging me.

The shrunken orange shape wobbled innocently, about twenty feet down, looking as easy to retrieve as a coin at the bottom of a swimming pool. I was a little comforted by knowing that sharks, especially tigers, got sort of nonchalant about getting themselves hooked. They had a why-fight-it attitude and just swam around with the hook in their mouth waiting for something to happen. But I also knew that their will to fight was not in the least diminished. Sharks don't understand what it means to give up.

I hated going in without a face mask. Everything beyond a few feet was blurry. I paused just below the skiff and looked around, all the way around. No giant moving shapes. The float wasn't as far down as it had appeared and I reached it in a matter of seconds. I pulled on it, and it gave.

I looked all the way around again. Nothing. Don't worry. Uncle Raz said that sharks were like dogs, lots of them around but they don't usually attack people. But not to worry wasn't part of me. I was as tight as an *opihi* sucked onto a rock in the surf.

Then something swept over the shapes on the ocean floor, a shifting of patterns. My stomach moved in a wave, and I felt a deep chill run through me as if I'd drifted over a freshwater spring. A huge, dark mass rose from the coral below. Even with blurred vision I could see that we'd hooked a shark, and a big one.

I felt for an instant as though I had no energy in me, like in a nightmare when something's after you and you can't get away fast enough.

The shape circled out. I had to move. I *had* to.

I let go of the float and raced upward, clawing the water, my heart pounding.

"*Pull me in!*" I gasped as I broke the surface next to the skiff.

Keo grabbed my arm and the back of my shorts. I kicked and pulled, and rolled over the gunwale with visions of leaving a leg in the jaws of the shark.

"What is it?"

"We got one . . . shark . . . big shark . . ." I caught my breath and started the engine. The float popped up. I squeezed one hand around the throttle so Keo couldn't see it shaking and gripped the side of the skiff with the other to hold my body still. Keo moved to the bow and lay on it with his arms outstretched and grabbed the float as we went by. I cut to neutral, still breathing hard.

"Now what?" I asked.

"We pull the anchor and take him home."

It was a great plan—it just didn't work. The anchor was so well wedged into the crevice that we couldn't get it out again without diving down and removing it by hand. And neither of us was dumb enough to suggest the coins for *that* one.

"Okay," Keo said after a minute or so of staring at me, and then into the water. "No problem. We'll just bring the old man out here."

I concentrated on calming my body. "How," I asked, but really didn't care. That I was out of the water was all that was on my mind.

"In the skiff."

"He works all day on the barge and you think he's going to take a ride out here?"

Keo thought for a minute. My body settled down. The float tugged at Keo's hands and he threw it back into the water. It sank, then reappeared.

"When he hears we got a big shark on the line, he'll come see. Why would they give a hundred bucks for a shark if they didn't want to see it?"

We rode back to the harbor with only the drone of the outboard and the slap of the hull on the water to break the silence.

There were always so many people around the old man that we couldn't get anywhere near him to tell him about the shark. When we asked Uncle Raz if he could think of a way for us to talk to him, he laughed. "You can see him in the movies."

Keo said nothing to Uncle Raz about the shark so I kept quiet about it too. Now that Uncle Raz was important he didn't have too much time to fiddle around with other things.

Keo and I went out to the end of the pier and sat down on the edge with our feet dangling over the water.

"I got an idea," Keo said, his eyes pinned on something unseen beneath the surface of the ocean. He was in one of his thinking trances. "The shark will die if we leave him out there too long. . . ."

I nodded. "Couple of days at the most."

Keo bit at his lower lip. When he grabbed on to something he was like the old man fighting sharks away from his marlin and he wasn't about to let up until he won, or flat out lost.

"I got it, I got it!" he yelled with a slap to his leg. "The box lunches! Uncle Raz takes the sixty box lunches out to the barge every day, right? Well, the old man gets one of those lunches."

"Okay," I said, but didn't get it.

"We put a note in every box lunch, the same note." Keo stood up.

"But everyone else will see it, too," I said.

"All the better. If he doesn't eat, all the notes will give everyone a good laugh. We can't miss."

We spent two secret hours that night writing sixty notes and folding them into little squares. Each note said:

> *Dear old man,*
> *We are Keo and Sonny. We have a shark for*
> *you. Look for us at 5:30 in the night after you*
> *work. We will be standing under the fish scale.*

The next morning we rode with Dad to the pier and volunteered to scrub Uncle Raz's boat down before the movie people came to go out to the barge. Dad took his sampan out fishing. Uncle Raz drove his truck over to Kona Inn to pick up the lunches. When he returned we offered to load them onto the boat.

"Okay with me," he said, "but don't you think I'm going to let you two ride out to the barge. Too many people already."

"That's okay, Uncle," Keo said. "We just want to help."

Uncle Raz went down into the bilge to check the engines. Keo and I slipped a note under the lid of each box as we removed them from the truck.

"If this doesn't work," I said, "we'll have to let the shark go."

"It'll work."

At five-thirty we were waiting under the fish scale as the movie people returned. Two movie guys came by and said hello to us, and smiled. The old man was in the last boatload to arrive.

We shooed away a handful of small kids that were nearby, not wanting them to obstruct the old man's line of vision. All he had to do was look up and he'd see us. He got off the boat and was immediately surrounded by a crowd of people. I thought he glanced our way but couldn't tell for sure. In seconds he was engulfed in a sea of heads. I stood up on my toes, and Keo climbed the fish hoist pole a few feet, then waved his arm.

The boss of the movies came over and broke up the crowd. The old man's hat moved along the top of the heads, like a sand crab skirting along the beach.

"Hey!" Keo yelled, but no one seemed to hear him. The old man took off his hat and got into the back of a car. He didn't even look over at us.

The next day Keo and I took Dad's skiff back to the point. The shark was still alive, but weak. For a moment Keo sat there with the wire cutters in his hand, staring at the cable. The shape of the shark wobbled below the skiff. I felt it, too, the moment of truth, as Uncle Raz would say, the moment you know you've won or lost. A hollow slapping sound slipped out from under the hull when Keo leaned over the side to cut him loose.

He clipped the cable quickly and threw it overboard. "Go on, get out of here," he shouted at the shark.

We waited ten minutes for it to leave the area before diving for the anchor.

"There goes a hundred bucks," Keo said.

"What would we do with it anyway."

"Yeah. What."

We both sat there staring into the water. As much as I wanted to be miles from any shark, I hated to see this one go.

When the old man came in from the barge later that day, he was standing on the stern deck of the *Optimystic* with his hands on his hips, balancing on the moving boat like a deck-hand. Keo and I sat on the hood of Uncle Raz's truck watching everyone on the pier rush over in a clump to catch a glimpse of him.

Two men cleared a space for him to get off the boat. The crowd stepped aside and clapped as he came ashore. He took off his hat and half-waved, then got into the long, black car that waited for him every afternoon. As the car passed, we could see him looking at us through the dark backseat window.

Then the car stopped, and backed up. The old man lowered the window. "You the two who sent me the note? The one in all those lunch boxes?"

We both slid off the truck like ice chips off the side of a cold bottle of beer. "Yeah," said Keo. "We sent the note. Did you see it?"

"How could I miss it?" The old man shook his head, then laughed, as if remembering something funny.

"We were at the fish scale," Keo said.

"I know," he said, throwing a hand up. "I saw you there. Do you have any idea how hard it is for me to get a moment to myself?"

Some of the people in the crowd noticed that his car had stopped and started walking toward us.

"Listen," he said. "I want to see your shark. Meet me right here at six in the morning, then take me to it. Can you do that?"

"We can be here at six, mister, but we can't show you the shark. We had to let him go or he'd die."

The old man scratched at his beard, under his chin, and thought for a minute. "Not much we can do now, then, is there? What was it about the shark you wanted me to see?"

Keo's face brightened. I couldn't believe his luck. He waved his hands around as he talked, first pointing to the fake sharks in the fenced-in area, then generally out to sea. He went on and on about how everything was too fake, and how sharks turn over on their sides when they bite into something that far out of the water.

The old man studied me, then Keo. He looked tired, more like he should have been sitting on the seawall with a fishing pole than in a big car with bodyguards.

I thought Keo had said too much. But the old man smiled and shook his head. "You any relation to Sturges?" he asked Keo.

"Who?"

"My director."

Keo shrugged no.

"How about a guy named Hemingway?"

Keo looked confused, but you could tell he was giving it serious consideration.

The old man's shoulders moved as he put his head down and laughed silently, to himself.

The small crowd of people closed in on us, stopping at the end of the car. The old man looked back at them. He puffed his cheeks up and let the air out slowly. Then he smiled at us. "You boys are okay," he said, giving us a short salute. "Thanks for the tips, I'll give what you told me some thought."

He winked and sat back in the seat. The window went up,

smoothly. The car passed through the gate and turned right. Its black roof, just visible above the top of the seawall, slid back through town toward the hotel.

Two days later Dad, Uncle Raz, and Uncle Harley sat on the end of the pier with Keo and me. Again, the old man was out in the skiff sitting with his elbows on his knees waiting for the sharks. This time the marlin was three-quarters eaten. The other two sat side by side on the pier like two giant canoes.

Uncle Raz waved a beer around as he pointed everything out to us. "This is the part where the sharks finish off the old man's fish," he said. "It's a shame. It was a nice one."

Dad laughed, but I didn't think Uncle Raz meant it as a joke.

"Quiet on the set," a man behind us yelled. The crowd of people hushed down until it was completely silent. Someone coughed. Uncle Raz scowled and turned to see who it was.

"Action!" The sharks jerked a little when they started, but moved smoothly as soon as they had gone a few feet. The old man stood up, this time with a club.

"Come on, *galanos*," he said. "Come in again!"

The sharks headed for the marlin and the old man beat down on the one closest to him.

"Cut!" shouted the voice from the crowd.

"Still looks fake," Keo said, shaking his head.

"They only use a small part of that," Uncle Raz said. "They mix it in with shots of real sharks."

The old man sat back down in the skiff. He took off his hat and glanced over at the people on the pier. When he saw Keo and me he waved and smiled. Dad put his hand on my shoulder. Uncle Raz thought the old man was waving at him and waved back.

The boss of the movies puttered out to the old man in a

fiberglass skiff and began talking to him. The two sharks swam backward, back out to sea.

"I saw you boys talking with the old man a couple of days ago," Uncle Raz said. "You were lucky to be in the right place at the right time. He's a hard man to get to see, let alone talk to."

"We had a shark to show him," Keo said, "but we had to let it go. We wanted to tell him about sharks so he would know what to do in that skiff when they make the movie."

"And he could see how they turn over when they bite a floating fish," I added.

"Hah!" Uncle Raz said. "Do you two know how many of those buggers they got on a line out at the barge? He's been looking at sharks for weeks. He doesn't need to hear about them from you."

I looked at Uncle Raz, surprised. Keo just kept on staring at the old man.

The boss came back to the pier.

"Look how fake it looks next time the sharks come in," Keo said. "If there are sharks out at the barge he must not have seen them."

"Boy, you crazy," Uncle Raz said. "That old man is a famous movie star. He knows what he's doing. What do you think *you* can tell him that he doesn't already know?"

Keo kept staring out in the direction of the skiff. He was as stubborn as Uncle Raz.

"Quiet on the set."

As the sharks attacked the old man's marlin yet once again, I watched him stand against them. His khaki pants were wrinkled and baggy, his shirt torn. The club rose and fell pathetically into the ocean, into the last moments of the hopeless battle. It is now, I thought, that he knows it's over. He's tired. The sharks will win. I could still see the cables, and the sharks looked stiff, like rubber pontoons. But this time I hardly noticed them. The movement of the club, rising and falling over and over and over, held me spellbound, like watching Dad, tense and grimacing, clubbing a shuddering *abi* that refused to die. The old man captured me in a way I couldn't explain. Some invisible power commanded all of my attention, like the blurry mass rising beneath me from the illusion of a stable ocean floor.

The boss of the movies let the camera run, and the old man kept striking aimlessly at the shapes in the water, until he fell to his knees and mumbled a last few brokenhearted words to the ravaged marlin. The crowd on the pier was dead silent. It was as if everyone had stopped breathing.

"Cut." The boss's voice trailed out over the water. The old man rested on his knees in the bottom of the boat. No one said a word.

Except Keo.

"The cables," he whispered, shaking his head.

The old man came back to the pier in a boat with the boss. The crowd broke up slowly, in whispers and low murmuring.

I walked home, because I wanted to be alone for a while. By the time I finally got there, the sky had turned a dark blue-black. The kitchen light cast its warm yellow out into the yard. Dad was frying hamburger, the smell pouring out the window. Steam rose around him as the frying pan popped and hissed.

Before going into the house, I went out to the rocks and sat on the edge of the island. The glow from the fading sunset left a warm, golden trail over the dark ocean that ended at my feet, as if I were connected to a great, glowing well just beyond the limits of my vision. The steady rush of waves sounded like the drone of Dad's sampan cruising out to the fishing grounds. The last of the sunset was so brilliant, in a muted sort of way, that I picked up a stone and threw it out to sea. I wondered if the old man was watching the night fall and tracing the same burning curves that cradled the undersides of clouds just above the horizon. He, too, would be standing at the end of the slowly fading trail of light.

The old man worked off the end of the pier for three more days, but Keo and I stayed up the hill with the dogs, shooting BB guns. Keo had seen enough. The whole thing was a waste of time, he said. The movie would look fake.

And I'd seen enough, too. Enough to know that this time, Keo was dead wrong.

4

The Year of the Black Widows

(1958)

Jack Christensen, the new boy from California, had convinced Keo and the rest of the sixth grade boys that they'd be in a bargeload of trouble when they went to the big school up in the highland jungles and had to deal with the seventh and eighth graders. Keo, being a year ahead of me, was the first to have to face the unknown—the shadowy school ten miles up the mountain, a place that suddenly loomed before us like a long, gray squall moving in from the sea.

Dark as it all seemed, though, it existed only in our minds. There were rumors and distorted facts passed down from older brothers and sisters, but no one really knew. Except Jack. He'd never been to the school and hadn't known anyone who'd gone there, but still, he knew, because he'd seen it all in Los Angeles. They smoke and drink and fight, he said. They join gangs and carry knives.

No one wanted to believe him, but there wasn't one of us who could ignore him. We'd form our own gang, he told us, and call it the

Black Widows. Any sixth grader who wanted protection could have it. All he had to do was swear to help any other Black Widow who got into trouble—and, Jack added, do whatever he said.

One morning in April I walked into the school yard and found Mrs. Carvalho, the principal, lowering a dead mongoose down the flagpole. Almost all eighty-seven kids in the school were standing around watching her. The mongoose was tied to the halyards by its tail.

Keo, Jack, and four other boys sat watching the whole thing from the steps leading up to the veranda that fronted our L-shaped, four-room schoolhouse. Bobby Otani, a fifth grader, sat next to Keo, trying to keep from laughing. But the others, all sixth grade Black Widows, were stone-faced. I went over to join them.

"What's going on?" I asked.

Keo ignored me. Bobby Otani snickered and Keo elbowed him. I sat on the lower step, below Keo. Mrs. Carvalho untied the mongoose and marched toward us, its tail pinched in her handkerchief. The mass of kids stepped aside as she moved through them. "Which one of you did this?" she asked.

I quickly stared down at my feet, realizing how guilty we must have looked, sitting off from everyone like we were. And it surprised me to find myself being accused along with everyone else. The younger kids gathered around Mrs. Carvalho and gazed up at us.

Immediately, the boys behind me said, one after the other, "Not me, Mrs. Carvalho; we didn't do it; not us."

Mrs. Carvalho searched our faces with narrowed eyes. "I want *all* of you in my office after school." She walked up the stairs past us, still holding the mongoose, the entire school following her. Some of the fifth and sixth grade girls smirked as they went by.

When Mrs. Carvalho was out of sight, Bobby Otani burst out laughing. Keo stood, and moved away from him with a disgusted look on his face. Bobby, like me, wanted to be in the Black Widows, but Jack wouldn't let any fifth graders join unless they proved to him that they wanted it bad enough. Jack was thinking of a test. He'd make us do something we didn't want to do, something that proved our loyalty.

Now Jack came down the stairs and grabbed Bobby by the shoulder of his shirt. "If you want to die before the sun goes down, just keep it up."

Bobby sobered. "Okay, okay." Jack's glare sliced through him, then the rest of us, wild with anger. Bobby pushed at Jack's hand, still gripping the shirt, but Jack stopped him with another glare. No one said a word. Then Jack went up and slouched across the veranda to the classroom, with the rest of us following in silence.

Keo put his hand out and stopped me. "Jack says the mongoose was a warning. Someone from the high school put it there to remind us who's boss." Then Keo sniggered. "Bobby thinks Jack put it there himself."

"Did he?"

"Who knows?"

Mrs. Lee, the fifth and sixth grade teacher, shook her head as we walked in, then started class as if nothing had happened.

One thing about Jack Christensen was that you could never outdo him. No matter what you told him, he'd seen or done it one better. He knew more, lots more. He came from the mainland, a place the rest of us could barely even imagine. He'd moved to the islands from California just before the school year started. Dad said his mother and stepfather were like a lot of people—they come to the islands thinking life will be easy, then find out that it's just as full of problems as anywhere else.

We gave Jack the nickname of Jack da Lolo, meaning Jack the Crazy, because he was peculiar-crazy, a real odd duck, as Uncle Raz liked to call him. But Uncle Harley thought Jack was lonely. Keo and I argued against that opinion but Uncle Harley just told us we were too young and too caught up in the boy to see it.

Keo and I liked Jack because he was always surprising us, and we hung around with him just to see what he'd do or say next. He had the power to hold us speechless with the things he told us, like all the stuff about the seventh and eighth graders. And he had the advantage of being taller than anyone else in school, at least two inches taller than me, and one taller than Keo. He never went barefoot to school like the rest of us but always wore black tennis shoes and jeans and a T-shirt with the sleeves rolled up. His hair was usually greased back, with a clump hanging down over his forehead. He was Keo's age, but seemed older because of his size, and because he knew so much more about the world than we did.

"Just wait till next year," he told Keo. "You'd better learn to protect yourself because you're going to get into a lot of fights in the seventh grade." All Jack's talk pulled Keo under, like a whirlpool. You could see it on his face, and in his eyes, and in the two vertical scowl lines between his eyebrows.

When school let out Mrs. Carvalho made all seven of us sit along one wall of her office. Everyone had gone home except the teachers. She glared across her desk at us for several minutes before saying anything, looking as if she were trying to determine which one of us had the nerve to run the mongoose up the flagpole.

"I know one of you boys put that mongoose up there," she finally said. "And I know that you *all* know who it was, because you have that guilty look on your faces."

We sat there staring at the floor.

"Bobby Otani," she said. "What do you know about this?" Mrs. Carvalho was pretty smart, going straight to the one most likely to tell her what she wanted to know. But Bobby just shrugged his shoulders.

She asked each of us the same question and got nothing but shrugs, and silence, or a whispered "I don't know." Then she made us sit for about twenty minutes while she worked at her desk, as if we weren't there at all.

Just as I was about to doze off, Mrs. Carvalho stood up. "Okay, boys," she said. "You can go, but I want you to remember that I'll be keeping my eyes on you." As we started to leave, she tipped her head toward Jack and added, "You boys should be setting a better example for our new student."

A few weeks later, just after midnight on a Saturday night, Jack stole his stepfather's car and picked up Keo, then Bobby Otani, then me. When Jack had learned that none of us ever *snuck out* at night, he couldn't believe it. In California *everyone* sneaks out, he said, then told us to be on the road in front of our houses at midnight.

With the dogs all standing around watching me, I climbed out of my bedroom window, just as Jack had told me to do. Dad was asleep in the living room. I could hear his breathing through the wall. I wore shorts and a sweatshirt, though the night air at sea level was still warm.

Jack's stepfather's car was a brand new green Oldsmobile four-door that reflected moonlight off its shiny hood as it approached, lights flashing off and on as a signal. The road went black when Jack pulled up and turned off the headlights.

Keo sat in front with Uncle Harley's twenty-two. Bobby was in the back. He stuck his head out the open window. "Come on, get in," he said, almost whispering. Keo and Jack kept quiet. I slid in next to Bobby, and Jack turned the car around in our driveway. I wondered what Dad would say if he found out what I was doing.

"Where we going?" I asked.

"Shoot rats," Jack said. "At the dump."

"You don't want to be up at the dump at night without a gun," Bobby said. "I heard there's a crazy man living there, but no one has ever seen him. He hides in the day and only roams the dump at night, looking for food. Isn't that right, Keo?"

"That's what I heard," Keo said.

If Keo had heard it, I would have heard it, too, and I hadn't. Still, it could be true. Who knew what went on up there? The dump was a strange enough place in full daylight. Something was always moving around—birds, rats, wild cats and starved dogs, mongooses. Why not a crazy man?

"Where'd you learn to drive?" I asked Jack.

"It's easy. The car's automatic, they're always automatic. That's what my stepfather likes. Anyone can drive this thing."

"He knows you drive it?"

"Sure."

"Does he know you have it now?"

"Of course not."

"It's more fun to steal it," Keo said, sounding as if he'd known Jack for years.

"It's not stealing," Jack said. "I just borrowed it for a while."

Keo sat like an army guard, holding the twenty-two straight up, butt on the floor, like a flagpole. He glanced out the window on his side of the car as if driving around in the middle of the night were something he did all the time.

I leaned forward with my arms on the back of Keo's seat, peering into the beams of light exposing the old road up to the dump. We were like a small band of outlaws heading for a crime, the four of us riding silently. Getting caught wasn't even a passing concern. I felt invincible.

Jack drove slowly into the dump, a huge, sloping, rectangular area carved out of the jungle of trees on the side of the mountain, far enough away from the village so you couldn't smell it. Carefully he snaked his stepfather's spotless car around broken glass and watery mud holes. The smell of the dump was different in the cool night air, not sickly like it was in the heat of the day, but sharp and biting.

Just above the dump itself was a flat area wide enough to turn a truck around. The dump flowed downhill in heaps and rolls. Jack parked the car on the edge of the turnaround, facing the downward slope, and turned off the headlights, then the engine. We waited a moment, listening to night noises coming up from the moonlight-gray field of garbage below.

"You got the flashlight?" Jack asked.

Keo flicked it on and sent a beam down to an old refrigerator lying on its side. Then he turned it off and with a length of fishing line strapped it to the barrel of Uncle Harley's rifle.

"What are you doing that for?" Bobby asked, as excited about being at the dump as a dog in a Jeep.

"So we can see what we're shooting at, what do you think?"

We got out of the car and stood on the edge, looking down into the ghostly mounds, black trees all around, a bright ring of illuminated mist around the moon. Jack took the rifle from Keo and turned on the flashlight. The beam followed the path of his aim, first lighting up a bottle, then a tire. "Pow!" he said, then shut the light off. "Listen."

Things were alive and moving around below us, noises from the far corners, tin cans tipping over somewhere in the middle. Jack turned the light back on and aimed the rifle around the dump until the beam reflected the glassy eyes of a mongoose, frozen between steps, low to the ground and ratlike. Jack shot. The bullet winged it, and it squealed and flipped around a couple of times, then disappeared into the garbage.

We had to stay up on the dirt part because we were barefoot.

Jack wore his black tennis shoes but didn't want to go down into the dump alone. He put his hand on my shoulder. "Find a cat. This place is loaded with them." The beam flopped around in the trees as he handed me the rifle. Keo said he thought he'd seen one over to the left when Jack was running the light around.

"How about a bottle?"

"Don't be a sissy. Go on, shine the light around."

I moved the beam slowly over the mounds just below us, maybe the length of eight cars away, and found a mongoose.

"Go ahead," Jack said. "Take a practice shot."

It was an easy target, like the coffee cans Keo and I set up in the pastures around his house. The mongoose didn't squeal when I hit it, just fell into a small hump and didn't move.

"Good shot!" Keo said.

Jack didn't say anything. I kept the beam on the dead mongoose, its brown body looking like a pile of mud. I'd never killed an animal before. I felt sick to my stomach. In Kona everyone shot mongooses, even Dad. They were pests, they got into your garbage, into your garage, into your cooled trash fires, and made a racket under your house. Still, I felt like there was a hole in me and all the excitement of the night was quickly draining away.

"Now find a cat," Jack said. "You want to be in the Black Widows, don't you?"

"Sure," I said.

"Then your test is to shoot a cat."

"But . . ."

"A cat. Shoot one or forget about the Widows."

We spent an hour or so looking around for cats but only found more mongooses. Even the crazy man wasn't there, but that didn't stop Jack from trying to scare us with sudden moves, whispering things like, "What was *that*?"

Jack drove fast going back down to sea level, jabbering the whole way with Keo. I sat in the backseat hanging on to a grip on the door. Jack bet Keo he could drive through the village without getting caught and slowed when we dropped down toward the pier from Palani Road.

"I've got an idea," Jack said, half turning toward the back seat. "You two want to be Black Widows, right? Well, Sonny can go back up to the dump and shoot the cat. That should prove he wants to be in bad enough. And you, Bobby, can put it in a bag, and hide it in Mrs. Carvalho's office."

"What?" Bobby said. "I could get kicked out of school for that."

"Take it or leave it," Jack said. Keo kept quiet, as if it didn't matter to him one way or the other whether Bobby or I became Black Widows.

I thought the whole thing was stupid. "Why do *we* have to prove ourselves, and not you?" I asked.

"Because I'm the leader."

I sat back in the seat trying to figure out how everything had gotten so confusing since Jack had come to the island. Now Keo was a Black Widow, and almost a stranger.

Jack glanced over his shoulder as he drove. "Of anyone in this car, you should be begging to be a Black Widow."

"What do you mean?" I said.

"I mean Begging with a capital B, white boy."

My forehead tightened, my eyes closed to slits.

White boy?

"White," Jack went on. "As in you're gonna get your butt kicked in seventh grade. They don't like white boys up there."

Keo was dead silent, staring straight ahead. I wanted him to say something—that Jack didn't know what he was talking about—but he didn't. *White boy?* Is that how it was? Is that how Keo saw me? I was like Keo . . . wasn't I? He was darker, but wasn't I as Hawaiian as he was on the inside?

"White boy or Black Widow," Jack said with finality. "You choose."

We made it through town without getting caught, because there was no one around to catch us. The street was empty and pale under the few lights along the road. Bobby talked the whole way down to my house about what Mrs. Carvalho would do when she found the cat in her office.

Just before we got to my driveway, Jack pulled over to the side of the road and turned off the headlights. I got out and peered back into the car. Jack leaned forward, a shadowy silhouette staring past Keo at me. "Get the cat," he said.

Keo looked away when I caught his eye, and said, "See you."

Thick trees on either side of our rocky driveway reached out toward me, their night shadows swallowing up the moonlight. Beyond, the trail of the moon lay like a ribbon of silk on a quiet sea.

The dogs heard me and came trotting out. I crept into the house, past Dad, sleeping, and gently closed the door to my room. Except for the low hiss of the surf, the night was silent.

I sat on my bed and stared out the window, hearing the faint echo of Jack's command—*get the cat*.

A week later Grampa Joe drove down and picked up Keo, and then me, and took us back to his place to help out with his coffee orchard, a small, five-acre farm with about twenty-five hundred trees. He paid us fifty cents an hour when he needed help.

In the morning we spread rat poison around the edges of the orchard, then sprayed diesel oil in among the trees where weeds had started poking through. Later Grampa Joe wanted us to help him gather up and haul off some old boards and tires that had cluttered his yard for as long as I could remember. Tutu Max must have gotten after him.

At noon the three of us sat out in the yard, in a small grassy area, one of several flat terraces that stumbled down from the road above. Grampa Joe's whole place was on a hill, as was all of Kona, except down along the coast where I lived. The island itself was just the top of a deep undersea mountain rising out of the Pacific Ocean.

All morning I'd been thinking about how Keo had become so quiet and moody. Jack seemed to consume him, to consume all of us with his stories about high school, and with the fear and doubt that settled in behind them. "Forget that junk that Jack says," I finally told Keo.

"You don't know your brains from a dead jellyfish," he answered, staring me down with squinting eyes.

"So what are you boys up to at school?" Grampa Joe asked.

Keo shrugged, eating one of the tuna sandwiches Tutu Max had made for us. Grampa Joe turned to me, and I shrugged, too. He kept looking at me, waiting.

"Keo's a Black Widow," I finally said. "It's a gang."

Keo held the sandwich in one hand while he ate, staring off into the trees.

Grampa Joe took a drink out of an old, dented silver thermos, then peeked over at Keo. "What do Black Widows do?"

Keo shrugged again. "Nothing . . . just hang around."

Grampa Joe picked at the grass, then shook his head and laughed, once, like a *humph*. "Black Widows," he mumbled.

"I'm going to be one, too," I said.

"What do you mean, *going to be*?"

"I have to shoot a cat first, to prove I'm worthy."

"Sheese, are you kidding? Really? Shoot a cat? Whose stupid idea was that?" He glanced at Keo, but Keo just kept on eating his sandwich.

"A boy named Jack," I said. "He's the leader. It was his idea to make the Black Widows."

Grampa Joe watched me, waiting for more. "Shoot a *cat*?" Keo glared at me.

I looked down at the grass, thinking I'd better not say too much more. "A cat," I said, almost in a whisper.

"You want cats? We'll see lots of them when we take this junk to the dump," Grampa Joe said. "No loss if you shoot one, but what a stupid idea. What does that prove? Nothing. Only that you can shoot." He turned to Keo. "Did you have to shoot one, too?"

"No."

"He's a sixth grader," I said. "So is Jack."

Grampa Joe nodded, then shook his head and continued eating his lunch in silence, curling his blackened, diesel-oil-covered fingers around the white bread of his sandwich as if they were as clean as the inside of a mango.

On the way to the dump Grampa Joe stopped by Keo's house so we could get the twenty-two. Boards stuck out of the back of the old car, the trunk wide open. Grampa Joe didn't even bother to tie it down. We'd have to make two trips, there was so much stuff.

The dump was quiet when we got there, no other people around. But the dogs were out, skittish, bone-sided, emaciated creatures poking around down near the lower end. Mongooses were everywhere, scurrying from cover to cover, long and sleek, with ratty tails the length of their bodies. After we emptied out Grampa Joe's trunk, Keo took some shots at them, hitting nothing. The noise scared the dogs off, but they slunk back when the shooting stopped.

"Sonny," Grampa Joe said, pointing off to the right at a spot halfway down, away from the dogs and mongooses. "A cat. Hard to see right now. Wait a minute," he said. "She'll move."

I squinted into the sun, then shielded my eyes with my hand. The cat moved, a spotted one, mostly orange and black, looking like it was stalking something. It picked its paws up slowly, one at a time, and held them in the air before each step.

Keo handed me the twenty-two. I climbed down off the edge and picked my way through the debris, this time with a pair of thongs on my feet. Grampa Joe and Keo squatted low to the ground behind me, watching.

Like the mongoose, the cat was an easy target. I followed it in the notch, the bead on its shoulder. The wooden stock against my cheek was sun-warm and the casing smelled of clean oil, even through the stench of the dump. I could have shot and joined the Black Widows immediately.

But I moved the barrel a fraction of an inch to the left and fired, missing by a foot. The cat jumped, then disappeared into the field of decaying camouflage.

"You pantie," Keo said, standing up.

Grampa Joe stayed down on his heels, laughing silently and shaking his head, as if he'd known all along that I'd never shoot the cat.

I shrugged, and said, "Missed."

"No kidding," Keo said, crossing his arms and turning his head to the side to spit.

Grampa Joe picked up a stick and creaked himself up, then stepped down off the edge. He poked around in the garbage and came up with a rancid-smelling ribbon of something that looked like squid. "Use this," he said, holding it out to me on the end of the stick. "Set a trap. Bombye she come back—and Keo and I come back, too. Next load. You wait here, she come back."

After the car had bounced out to the main road I picked my way down to where the cat had been. I found it in a small cave formed in the folds of a pile of cardboard boxes. Its eyes flashed out at me, like coins wrapped in cellophane. It wasn't alone.

Four multicolored kittens shrunk back next to it as I peeked in. The mother hissed at me, and tolerated my being there as long as I didn't move around. I squatted down and watched them, holding as still as the old refrigerator.

After a while the kittens began to get restless, creeping slowly out of the shadows into the sun. Though wary of me, they got braver, jumping over each other and spreading out around the mouth of the cave. The mother stayed where she was, her front feet tucked up under her.

I laid the squid an arm's length away, moving as slowly as I could. Three of the kittens came over to sniff at it, one by one. The fourth wouldn't get anywhere near it. But one of the three brave ones inched its way around the squid, coming within reach, as if it had forgotten I was there, a dirty white one, with a splatter of black and orange spots on it.

The kitten sniffed at the squid then licked it enough to see that it wasn't fit to eat and turned its head away. Very slowly I reached out and pinched it at the back of its neck. The other kittens ran back into the cave.

Curled up and hanging from my fingers, it was as light as a plumeria lei. It struggled a little, but mostly just stayed curled up, its eyes stretched back, probably scared spitless.

I pulled my T-shirt over my head with my free hand and slipped it down my arm, then pulled the cat's head through the sleeve. I wrapped the rest of the shirt around its body, a wad of T-shirt with a scrubby cat's head poking out. It hissed when I let go of its neck.

When Keo and Grampa Joe returned, I was sitting on a wooden chair that I'd found. The kitten had gotten used to me by then. I stroked its head to calm it, but kept it wrapped in my T-shirt. Keo's twenty-two lay on the ground next to the chair.

Grampa Joe laughed when he saw the kitten. "The cat shrunk," he said.

"There are three more of these down where the big cat was."

Grampa Joe shook his head and started taking the junk out of his trunk. Keo came over and bent down to scratch the kitten's ears and got a hiss for it. "It's got to get to know you first," I said.

"What are you going to do with it?" he asked.

"I don't know. Keep it."

"What for?"

I shrugged.

"What about Jack?"

"He said to get a cat."

"He said to *shoot* a cat," Keo said.

"I know, but maybe he'll change his mind."

Keo stood up. "Jack? He won't. Only your shooting the cat will prove anything to him. You have to do it just like he says."

"Do *you* do everything he says?"

Keo picked up his rifle. "He hasn't told me to do anything yet."

"But if he did, would you? If he told you to shoot a cat, would you?"

"Easy."

"Okay, then. How about a dog? Would you shoot one of those?" I said, pointing to the dogs nosing around in the bottom of the dump. Keo loved dogs. If he said yes, he'd be lying.

"Stupid question. I'm already a Black Widow. I don't have to do anything." Keo took his rifle to the car.

By the time Grampa Joe dropped me off at my house the kitten was getting pretty antsy about getting out of the T-shirt. Grampa Joe told me I'd better soak the shirt in alcohol after carrying a mangy, flea-infested dump cat around in it. His arm hung down the side of the car door, the engine idling.

"Listen," he said. "I've known lots of guys like this Jack, who like to talk big and make you scared. Sometimes they were mean pachooks, that's for sure. But most of the time they were all smoke and no fire. Don't let him make you do something you don't want to do." Then he scratched the kitten's head and backed out to the main road.

When Dad came home from fishing, he found me sitting on the steps leading up to the porch, introducing the kitten to the dogs. I'd tied a length of nylon fishing line around its neck, like a leash, so it wouldn't run off and get killed by a mongoose. The dogs were curious, inching up to sniff at it, but holding off when the kitten hissed at them.

Dad asked where I'd gotten it, and I told him the whole story. His eyes narrowed when I told him Jack wanted me to shoot a cat to prove I was worthy to join the gang.

"Is Keo going along with all this?" he asked.

I nodded. "He's already a Black Widow."

Dad stood in the yard looking up at me with his hands on his hips, wearing only shorts with shiny dried fish slime by the pockets from wiping his hands on them. "So, you were going to shoot a cat because you wanted to be a member of Jack's gang?"

I nodded.

"Did Keo shoot one?"

"He didn't have to. He's a sixth grader."

"What about Jack?"

"He winged a mongoose."

"Everyone shoots mongooses," Dad said. "But cats?" He paused a moment, then went on. "Why do you want to be a part of this gang, anyway?"

"For protection. Jack says we're going to get into a lot of fights with the seventh and eighth graders. He says they carry knives."

"You believe that?"

I shrugged. "I guess so."

Dad stared at me, as if trying to read my thoughts. "Do you think your Uncle Harley and I would let you and Keo go to a school where the kids carried knives?"

I thought about that a moment, then shrugged and said, "I don't know." It had never entered my mind that Dad or Uncle Harley ever even thought about what we did at school, except ask us how our grades were once in a while.

Dad started up the steps, and put his hand on my shoulder as he passed. "If Sonny Mendoza can shoot this cat, or any cat, then I don't know a thing about my own son." He nudged my head with his hand. "Take that scrubby rat and soak it in the ocean until all the fleas float off, then you can bring it inside the house."

On Monday I left home later than usual and walked slowly so I'd arrive at school just as it was starting and wouldn't have to talk to Jack until recess.

I'd made a small dome-shaped pen out of chicken wire and staked it into the yard, a place for the cat to stay while it was getting used to its new home. I figured out that it was a female, and decided to call her *Popoki*, Hawaiian for cat. When I left the dogs were lying on the grass nearby watching her with droopy tongues, panting.

At recess, Keo came up to me before going outside. "How's the cat?"

"Okay."

"Jack's expecting to see it, a *dead* cat. He doesn't know you have a live one."

"So."

"So nothing. Just reminding you."

Keo stared me in the eye a moment, then strolled off with the same disgusted look on his face he'd given Bobby Otani.

I stayed in the classroom. Keo went out to join the Black

Widows under *their* tree, a billowing monkeypod that Jack had commandeered as their meeting place. Only Black Widows and invited guests could sit under it.

Mrs. Lee asked me if I was feeling all right, and I told her that I was. She sat on a desk and studied me. "After as many years as I've taught fifth grade boys, Mr. Mendoza, you can't tell me that nothing is bothering you. A boy *never* stays inside at recess unless he's sick, it's raining, or he has a problem."

I told her a lie and a truth. Everything was okay at school, but I was worried about my new cat. I told her I didn't want a mongoose to get it, then went outside before she could ask too many questions.

Keo, Bobby Otani, Jack, and four sixth grade Black Widows sat under the *Tree of Webs*, as Jack had started calling their meeting place, building more into his Black Widow idea every day. Three sixth grade girls sat with them.

"Hey," Jack called when I came out into the yard. "Where is it?" The girls and the Black Widows turned and looked over at me. Seeing Keo among the band of taunting eyes made me feel lost, as if I were in a strange school and he was just a boy I'd never seen before.

"I have it," I said.

"Good!" Jack said. "So show us?"

"It's at home."

Bobby Otani pinched his nose. "Must be getting ripe."

Jack stood and puffed up his chest, then strolled over to me, the group following him. "Black Widows!" he called, waving to the girls as well. "Come in close."

A low round of sniggering ran through them as they surrounded me. Keo held back a step, and mostly kept his eyes on the ground.

Jack went on. "Sonny wants to be a Black Widow, and we

want him to be one, too. So I gave him a test. Anyone who's not a sixth grader has to take a test." Jack peered into the eyes of everyone in the group, capturing their full attention. "If he .passes," he went on, "he's in. If he fails, he's out."

The Black Widows and the girls waited silently.

"His test was to shoot a cat at the dump and bring it to me in a box."

I think that startled the girls. All three of them moved closer. One opened her mouth to say something, but kept quiet, squinting her eyes as if Jack's order was so appalling she couldn't find the words.

"Tomorrow," Jack said, staring at me. "Bring it to school."

Keo shook his head when I glanced over at him. He must have been picturing Jack's reaction when he learned about the kitten.

The next morning I took Popoki to school in a small box, leaving late again, and walking into the classroom with everyone sitting at their desks watching me. Word had spread in whispers that I was bringing a dead cat to school. But within ten minutes the whole fifth and sixth grade knew there was nothing dead in the box at all, by all the noise the kitten made.

Even Mrs. Lee heard it, and came over to take a look. "It's so cute," she said, picking it up and showing the class. "I can see why you were so worried about it."

Jack refused to look at me the whole morning, acting as if I didn't exist. Keo kept to himself too, and so did the rest of the Black Widows.

At recess I took the box outside and was immediately surrounded by a horde of girls wanting to see the kitten. Jack and the Black Widows shoved their way through them. I stood holding the box with Popoki's head peeking through the slightly opened top.

"I said a *dead* cat, stupid." Jack glared down at me, looking as if I'd made a fool of him.

"Kill it."

A hush fell over everyone. No one moved or even dared to breathe. Keo, standing behind Jack, looked as serious as if he'd been told his dogs had run off. Jack reached for the box, and I jerked it away.

"You little punk," he said. He slapped the box out of my hands. When it hit the ground, the kitten stumbled out and rolled into a forest of feet, then sprinted away. I started after her, but Jack tripped me and fell on me, sitting on my stomach slapping at my face. "Sissy little punk," he said.

I turned from side to side, trying to dodge his hands, my arms pinned under his knees. I heaved up with my stomach, but he was too heavy. The stinging slaps turned into blows. One of them hit my nose and sent a pain through my head like I'd never felt before. I squirmed and twisted, but the blows kept coming, harder.

Then suddenly Keo slammed into Jack, knocking him off me. The ground shook when they hit. The Black Widows spread away, some of them saying, "Get him, Keo, get him."

I got up on my hands and knees, blood from my nose dripping down into the dirt. Keo and Jack rolled back and forth, their faces contorted, making spitting sounds. Jack pushed Keo away and scrambled to his feet. Before Keo could get up, Jack kicked him. Keo tried to slide away, but Jack kept going after him. I staggered over and hit Jack from behind and knocked him to the ground again.

"Boys! Stop it, *now*!" Mrs. Carvalho yelled, suddenly appearing, swatting at us with a yardstick.

I let go of Jack. He jumped up with his fists clenched, glaring at me with demon eyes.

"Sonny! Keo!" she said. "Go to my office! You should be ashamed of yourselves ganging up on Jack."

Then she turned to Jack. "Follow me."

"But I have to get my cat!" I said.

"*Not another word!*"

As Keo and I made our way through the crowd of kids, I saw Bobby Otani handing the cat to Mrs. Lee.

Dad was disappointed in me when he heard about the fight, especially since Mrs. Carvalho called him and asked that I stay out of school for three days. He took me out fishing with him, making me scrub the deck after every fish he caught. Keo just stayed home and shot at tin cans with the twenty-two. Jack had to stay away from school, too.

Mrs. Lee seemed genuinely pleased to see me when I returned and even asked about my cat. I told her she'd gotten to like the dogs and that no mongoose would even think of bothering her with them around. She patted me on the back and told me to try to stay out of trouble.

Jack now sat under the Tree of Webs alone. Only Mrs. Carvalho couldn't see his mean streak. But the rest of us stayed away from him, watching him from the opposite corner of the school yard. He usually spent the entire recess throwing a pocketknife into the ground, trying to get it to land blade down.

Around two weeks after the fight Mrs. Carvalho came into our classroom and asked Keo and me to please follow her outside. Everyone in the room watched us leave.

When we got out on the wide veranda, she searched our eyes. "You are excused from school for two hours," she said. Keo and I just stood there staring at her. Then she smiled and tipped her head toward the school yard. "Go with him."

Grampa Joe leaned up against the hood of his car with his arms crossed.

"What's going on?" Keo asked as we approached him.

"Nothing," he said. "I'm just taking you to lunch."

Keo and I looked at each other, then got into the car. Grampa Joe fired it up and drove us up the hill, to the highlands—to the high school.

"We're having lunch here," he said. "You know Herman Fukuoka? The guy with the coffee trees next to my place? His wife runs the kitchen."

"But why eat here?" Keo asked.

Grampa Joe tapped Keo's shoulder and said, flicking his eyebrows, "Good food."

The cafeteria buzzed with students, many of whom we knew from last year at the elementary school. A couple of them waved and came over to eat with us. The lunchroom was loud. Everyone seemed excited, but the guys who sat with us said it was like that every day.

I looked around to see how many white boys there were— only two. But no one was bothering them. They were just like everyone else.

The whole time we were there Grampa Joe kept quiet, just ate his lunch and listened to us talk with our friends. When lunch was over, he drove us back down to the elementary school, talking about his coffee trees all the way.

When we got out of the car, Keo said, "Why did you take us up to the high school for lunch?"

"I told you, good food," Grampa Joe said. "How's the flea-bag cat?"

"Fine," I said.

Grampa Joe nodded, then left.

Walking back up to the classroom, I kept thinking about the two white boys at the high school. Then it suddenly struck me that Jack was white, too. I don't know why I hadn't thought of it before. The Black Widows weren't *our* protection, they were his—Keo and all the other boys with dark skin and mixed blood. Jack Christensen was smart, all right. But I didn't care very much what Jack thought. It was what Keo thought that mattered.

After a while Jack, Keo, and I were talking again, but we never brought up the cat, or the Black Widows, or the fight. We didn't even talk about high school. But Jack did confess that he had tied the mongoose to the flagpole.

As the school year ended, Keo's worry changed into boldness. He was going to the big school next year. You could see it in the way he walked and the way he started holding himself more erect, pushing out his chest. He went to work for Uncle Harley that summer, weighing and buying fish from the charter boats, and from the small commercial boats, like Dad's, then selling them in Hilo.

Jack met us on the pier late one afternoon, to say good-bye. He told us his parents were moving back to California. Keo and I were sitting in Dad's Jeep, waiting for a ride home. Jack stood on Keo's side, still wearing jeans and a T-shirt with the sleeves rolled up, and greased-back hair. Our conversation was full of long silences, where each of us paused, and looked off somewhere.

"Hey," Jack said after one particularly long quiet spell. "Maybe you could start up the Black Widows again."

Keo nodded, staring straight ahead at the steering wheel with a blank look on his face. "Maybe," he said.

Beyond Jack the ocean was turning slightly pink. Waves thumped easily into the rocks on the other side of the small boat landing.

Jack pulled a pack of cigarettes out of his back pocket, something we'd never seen him with before. He tapped one out and stuck it in his mouth, then pulled a wooden stick-match from his front pocket. There was no breeze, but still Jack cupped his hands after striking the match on the side of Dad's Jeep. His cheeks sank as he sucked in. A cloud of smoke surrounded his face. Jack shook the flame out. His eyes watered, and he coughed.

"Nasty things," he said, taking the cigarette and hiding it in the palm of his hand, pinching it between his thumb and first finger. Then he pointed the pack of cigarettes at us and shook a few of them halfway out of the pack. Keo and I each took one. "Hey, look me up if you ever get to Los Angeles." Jack backed away, then turned and strutted off toward the seawall.

"Hey, Lolo," Keo called.

Jack turned, walking away from us backward. He smiled, and flipped us off, then went on. We both laughed. There was something about Jack that you just had to like.

I started to throw the cigarette away, but Keo said, "Wait! Give it to me. It's good for cleaning face masks, better than seaweed."

We sat in the Jeep watching Jack make his way along the seawall. Just before it ended he stopped and flicked what was left of his cigarette out into the ocean. You could see it twirl out in a graceful arc, spinning flawlessly into the water, as if he'd been smoking and flicking the butts away every day of his life.

5

Get Mister Red a Beer

(1959)

———

While Keo hauled fish with Uncle Harley that summer before seventh grade, I went to work as Uncle Raz's deckhand.

The *Optimystic*, Uncle Raz's sleek, white, forty-five-foot Chris-Craft charter boat, wasn't anything at all like Dad's ancient Japanese sampan. It was nearly twice as long and twice as smooth, fanning over swells like a water ski. The *Optimystic* had a hull of fiberglass and practically flew out to the marlin grounds under twin gas-powered Chrysler engines, instead of laboring under the weight of wood, and crawling along the coast on a single worn-out diesel.

Every year for five years straight a rich man from Bakersfield, California, had tied up Uncle Raz and his boat for a week-long charter in July. His name was Red, a big man with orange hair that never looked combed. For a week straight he poured beer and money into Uncle Raz like there was no end to it. Until now he'd always come with a couple of his friends, other loud men with stomachs for fishing drunk five days in a row. They'd caught at least one good-sized marlin every year, and despite all the drinking, not one of them ever seemed to feel the slightest bit queasy while they were out on the boat. Even Uncle Raz wondered how they did it.

This time, though, Red had brought along a new wife—his fourth, he didn't mind bragging—half his age and quiet as a coconut. Red called her Honey. Her skin was tanned and smooth, and she had flowing golden hair that she tied behind her while she lay in the sun.

This summer the fishing was slow, and Red hadn't caught anything. *Skunked*, as he called it. On his last day out he was as restless as Uncle Raz was rich. He brought aboard a banquet of new skin-diving gear, telling us that if nothing struck the lines by two o'clock, Uncle Raz was to anchor the boat close in, a few hundred yards offshore. "I came here to catch fish, by God, and I ain't going home with nothin' to show for it. If we got to go down there and catch 'em by hand, then that's damn well what we'll do."

"You're the boss, Red, you're the boss," Uncle Raz said. Then he turned to me and snapped, "Stow that gear, Sonny, and get Mister Red a beer."

It wasn't even seven in the morning.

We set out through the harbor about the time the rest of the charter boats were still idling at their moorings, skippers roaming their boats, sponging salt off the windows, bringing out the rods and fingering their secret lures. Red stood on the stern deck with his knees up against the transom.

I pulled my favorite big-game lure out and checked the leader and skirt for nicks—a straight runner with a center leader hole. We'd caught three marlin on it already.

"Don't use that one, boy," Red said. "It's no good. You got to pick just the right plug for these waters."

"Sonny," Uncle Raz called. "Let Red do that. You just bring the rods out."

Scowling, I followed Uncle Raz's orders. Right or wrong, I did what he said. I needed the job.

Honey settled down on the stern bunk. She gave me a funny look, as if she were amused.

I half-smiled back and turned away.

Uncle Raz headed south, slowly, so Red could get a look at the coves and small beaches along the shoreline.

Uncle Raz shook his head when I came into the cabin after setting the rods in their holders. "This place is dead, dead, dead!" he said.

We passed by the point at the far end of the bay where the new Hilton Hotel was going to be built. It looked like any other part of the coast, mostly kiawe and coconut trees, and scrub brush above a black lava-rock shore. The cove below was green and clear.

"Your aunty doesn't know what she's talking about," Uncle Raz said suddenly. The night before, we were all up at Keo's house talking about the news of the Hilton. "We have enough hotels already," Aunty Pearl had said. But Uncle Raz thought it was the best thing he'd heard in years.

"Look at that jungle of thorn trees," he said as we cruised by the point. "The hotel will turn that into something beautiful."

It wasn't at all clear to me why Aunty Pearl had gotten so upset about a new hotel going in. "Someday we going lose more than we get," were her exact words. "This is only the beginning."

Uncle Raz practically shouted at her. "Yes, it's only the beginning—of a much livelier place." He'd paced back and forth on the porch waving around a bottle of beer. "This coast will be *jumping* with tourists," he went on. "No place in the world is as good as the Big Island for marlin fishing. No place. When people find that out, we'll *all* be rolling in business."

Aunty Pearl listened, never changing the expression on her face. "They only want the money," she said when Uncle Raz was done. She'd said it softly, almost in a whisper.

Uncle Raz threw up his hands and walked away.

By now the sun was peeking over Hualalai and the trees on the point were backlit, glowing like motionless torches in the first heat of day. Uncle Raz edged close to the cove. Red walked in from the deck, beer in one hand and one of Uncle Raz's lures in the other, a flashy one that someone had given him. Uncle Raz said you couldn't catch a log with it.

Uncle Raz perked up and spoke a little louder so Red could hear him over the hum of the engines. "They're going to blast through that rock over there so they can get down into the cove and make a little beach."

Red dipped his head and scanned the point. In my mind I saw white-skinned tourists jumping off the rocks into the water, and striped towels spread along a man-made beach. The cove was full of swimmers and the ocean was murky from all the commotion. No more spear fishing in *that* spot.

Red turned away, and held up the lure. "Try this one," he said.

Uncle Raz smiled. "That's the one, Red."

It was a long boat ride to two o'clock, zigzagging our way out to the fishing grounds, then back toward the island, then back out to the grounds again.

Honey drank Cokes and lay around in the sun with her dark glasses and suntan oil. I caught her watching me a couple of times, still amused. As hard as I tried to keep from glancing at her, I couldn't. What was so funny?

Red was all over the place—out on the bow, up on the flying bridge, down in the bilge. "Come see these engines, Honey," he called once, but Honey just cocked her head and lifted her Coke.

Red told us he owned four bars now, clubs, he called them. "Honey used to dance at one of them," he said, "until she married me. Now she owns the damn place."

Uncle Raz smiled and shook his head. "Kailua is just a spit on the sidewalk compared to the mainland," he said. Uncle Raz was the only one in our family who'd ever even been there.

"You're right about that," Red agreed. "But Kona is good for marlin, at least most of the time. Fighting a fat swordfish is as good as bull riding. There's nothing like it."

"That's what I keep telling Sonny's daddy," Uncle Raz said, jerking his head toward me. "I don't know how he can sit around all day in a pack of small boats hoping to find a couple of tuna. *Marlin!* That's where *life* is at!"

At precisely two o'clock, Red snapped his fingers and pointed at Uncle Raz, who turned to me. "Sonny, bring in the lines." The reels hadn't clicked once in six hours.

Uncle Raz swung back toward the island.

We anchored off a long stretch of uninhabited shoreline in a small, turquoise shallow-water cove.

Red dug into the pile of new diving gear, tossing things out to me and Uncle Raz—fins, face masks, snorkels, and two high-powered spearguns. The three of us went aft and studied the shapes on the ocean floor below. The stern rose gently as mild swells rolled in to shore, the water clear to a depth of thirty or forty feet, a perfect day for diving.

"Come on in, Honey," Red said, sitting on the stern bunk near Honey's feet. Uncle Raz and I looked back at ourselves in the lenses of her silver-mirrored glasses. Red stroked one of her feet with his beefy fingers. "Come on," he said. "I bought you a nice pair of fins."

Honey gave him a sweet smile. "You boys go on," she said.

Red moved in and gave her a kiss. He was quiet for a moment when he pulled away, as if distracted by a thought. Honey put her hand on his, and he smiled back.

Red stood up quickly and put on his new fins and face mask, then picked up one of the spears and jumped over the transom into the ocean.

"Be careful," Honey called, but I didn't think Red heard her. Uncle Raz and I jumped in after him and put our gear on in the water.

The sea was warm, and I floated easily on its surface, staring down into the reef and listening to the hollow sound of my breathing echoing through the snorkel. It's funny how the whole world shifts when you take that first breath-stopping gaze under water. Any way you look at it, it's a completely new world, a place that shrinks you down, a huge aquarium with hundreds of different sea creatures, none of which seems to think you're anything special.

I took in a deep breath and followed Red and Uncle Raz to the bottom, popping my ears against the pressure as I dove deeper. The sandy areas were smooth, with no shell trailings. But there was a small school of fat *ulua* that we chased around a cave on the underside of a coral shelf. Uncle Raz speared two of them and took them back to the boat.

I floated like a log in deep sea, face down, breathing through my snorkel, daydreaming. The sun felt good on my back.

Suddenly Red frogged clumsily below and looked up, waving his hand for me to follow him. Then he came up for air. "Come," he gasped. "Come see . . . You won't believe this."

He led me over the top of a giant undersea formation forty feet down, a massive shelf of milky coral, looking like an ancient aquarian island-city for hundreds of fish—blue, green, yellow, even black. I'd never seen anything like it before, fish nibbling and darting around in waves, lolling in and out of a thousand deep cracks and sharp-cornered fissures.

I floated over it, still as a leaf, as if caught in a vivid dream that I didn't want to wake from. A deep circular shaft fell about fifteen feet farther into the center of the island, to a white sand bottom. And from mossy balconies in the wall of the descending hollow, a horde of sea life speckled over the coral, nibbling and pecking, feeding, paying no mind at all to the two of us lurking over them.

I looked up to find a landmark on shore, trying to fix our location as well as I could.

Red took a deep breath and dove down for a closer look at the hole in the coral island. He stayed there about a minute and a half, then came up and sucked in great gulps of air.

"You see . . . that black coral down there? . . . That's my prize . . . that's my marlin!"

I went down for a look of my own. At the bottom of the circular shaft grew a magnificent, complete, reaching head of black coral, framed within the well as if the whole place existed only to draw attention to this black jewel at its base.

Flawless.

When I came back up, Red seemed to be thinking about what to do next.

"Where's Raz," he demanded. I pointed to Uncle Raz's snorkel sticking out of the water closer to shore. "Get him," Red said.

I swam over to Uncle Raz and told him what Red had found. "It's beautiful . . . the most beautiful thing I've ever seen underwater." Then I added, "Red wants you—now."

Uncle Raz beat me over to Red by at least ten lengths. "Come on, come on!" Red said, waving Uncle Raz closer. "I want that coral, for Honey—she can put it behind the bar in one of the clubs."

"Let's take a look," Uncle Raz said, then went under, little puffs of air flowing from his snorkel as he glided down. I followed him.

Hand over hand Uncle Raz pulled his way down into the

well. Fish darted away as he approached, then turned, and watched from a distance. I moved, so I could see better, then dove deeper, tempted by the beauty of the fish, and the black coral. Red watched above, floating in watery space.

The pressure was strong and my ears ached. How Uncle Raz could go so deep was a mystery to me. He was the best diver of all of us.

Uncle Raz stopped when he got about three-quarters of the way down the hollow. I moved around to get a better look, diving farther into the well, and saw what had stopped him.

Inches away from his left arm a massive brown head protruding from a cave waved slowly back and forth, eyes pinned on Uncle Raz—a fat moray eel, undulating with its breathing, repulsive, cavernous mouth chewing the water.

Uncle Raz started to back out of the well. The eel's mouth opened and closed. You could see the line of needle-sharp teeth.

Then the head fired forward like a spear and bit Uncle Raz's arm savagely, between his wrist and elbow.

Uncle Raz reeled back in pain. He yelled, and bubbles rushed from his mouth. He must have wanted to yank his arm away, but he knew it would be useless. The eel would only bite deeper. Uncle Raz kept still, his mouth in a tight grimace. He needed a razor-sharp knife to hack himself free, to get up for air. But he didn't have one, only the spear gun, and he was too close to use it.

Most of the eel's long snakelike body was twisted into a coral cave, gripping the turns and twists with steel muscles.

He's going to die! Uncle Raz is going to die! I recoiled. Is this really happening? *Don't ever do that again, boy! You're not a baby anymore . . . Calm down, now.* The dream-memory. I kicked frantically around him, above him. I could do *nothing*.

But Uncle Raz was not one to panic. With an inner will I would never find within myself, he remained unbelievably calm. An eel needed to breathe. And like a fish, it would open its mouth to do that. It would bite again, but there would be an instant where the mouth would open.

When? Could Uncle Raz hold his breath that long?

I had to go up for air.

"What's going on?" Red asked when I burst into the open.

I gulped in acres of air and dove back down without answering. Uncle Raz's lungs must have been exploding.

Then the eel breathed and Uncle Raz broke free. He pushed to the surface, blood streaming a wet mist from his arm. I rose beside him.

"*Aahhh . . .*" he gasped as we hit the air. "*Damn*, that hurts!"

"What?" Red said, clearly irritated.

"*Puhi*," Uncle Raz said, his face pinched up in pain. "Damn eel bit me."

I was so scared I could hardly speak. Blood was turning the water brown around him. "You're bleeding badly," I finally said.

Uncle Raz gave me the speargun and held his wounded arm with his good hand. "S'okay . . . let it bleed . . . the teeth on those damn things are always contaminated with something . . ."

"Let's get to the boat and clean up your arm," Red said. "Then go back for that coral."

Silence.

"You can shoot it, or something," Red said.

Uncle Raz stared at Red. "Sonny," he finally said. "Come with me."

Uncle Raz and I swam back to the boat and climbed aboard. "Get the fish knife," he snapped, ripping his face mask off.

Honey sat up and lifted her glasses.

Uncle Raz reached into the fish box for one of the speared

ulua. I gave him the knife and he sliced several meaty slabs of its flesh into long strips and tied them together in the center with a length of fishing line.

"What are you going to do?" I asked.

"Mister Red wants the coral. We're going to get it for him."

"*What!* But . . ."

"He pays me well, boy. I do what he says, and you do what I say. You better pay attention if you want to run a charter boat, because this is how it's done. Go pull the anchor."

Uncle Raz fired up the engines and walked the boat over toward Red, the dual exhausts bubbling and gurgling with each roll of the hull. I waited on the bow for the signal to drop the anchor. Uncle Raz scowled through the windshield. His arm was full of holes and had to hurt like crazy. *He* was crazy to go back down there. He could have drowned!

When he nodded, I dropped the anchor, tested it, then went aft. Uncle Raz shut the boat down.

Honey watched in silence as Uncle Raz came out into the sun wrapping an old Ace bandage around his arm.

"Get my spear," he told me, then checked the tied strips of *ulua.* He took the spear and poked the point into the bundled mass of raw fish, then dropped back into the sea.

I was just about to jump in behind him when Honey called to me.

"Sonny. Don't be too hard on your uncle . . . It's not easy to say no to Red."

I glanced back at her, surprised. She'd never said a *word* to me. I didn't even know she knew my name.

"But he's a good man," she added. "Down inside he's a good man . . ."

I nodded and jumped overboard. He's okay, I thought. But he's still bossy.

Red and I sank down and watched Uncle Raz approach the

rim of the well, inching down into it with the *ulua* flesh wafting gently on the point of the spear. The cavern where we'd seen the eel was vacant—no eyes, no ugly head. I cringed, not knowing where it was.

Just then the eel poked its head out of the cave. Uncle Raz jerked back. The eel glared at us, keeping a wary distance, like one of Dad's hunting dogs growling and fanging a cornered pig. Uncle Raz moved the strips of raw fish closer. The eel followed the spear with its eyes. I could almost hear Uncle Raz's thoughts: *that's right*, puhi, *this is for you. Come get it, sweet meat.*

Uncle Raz held himself still, moving only the tip of the spear, slowly in small circles near the head of the eel. The moray watched the *ulua* flesh with chilling concentration. Then, without even a hint of warning, it attacked the meat, furiously sinking its pointed, pin-sized teeth in and ripping it off the spear. He slunk back into his cavern leaving his head out only a few inches, enough to keep an eye on Uncle Raz. More food than he knew what to do with hung from either side of his mouth.

Uncle Raz slowly backed out of the well, and together, the three of us rose to the surface.

Back on the boat, I wondered: what was the purpose in feeding the eel? I watched Uncle Raz work without asking any questions. He seemed pleased with himself.

"What about the coral?" Red said.

"As soon as I get rid of the eel, it's yours."

Uncle Raz took a large steel hook from the tackle drawer and tied it to the end of a spool of heavy fishing line. "Greed is going to make this *puhi* sorry," Uncle Raz said, punctuating each word with a stab of the hook. He smiled at Red and added, "No one's going back to California empty-handed."

In that moment Uncle Raz seemed like a kid, delighted with the brilliance of his plan and with the edge his intelligence gave him over the eel. "Time for part two," he said. "Let's go."

The moray was gorging itself on the *ulua*. Uncle Raz crept

down on him with the hook in his hand. The eel's jaw worked in sideward motions, not seeming to care much about what we were up to.

Uncle Raz brought the hook within inches of its head, and with slow, measured movements, brought it up under the jaw. The eel stopped moving its mouth. Uncle Raz held still until it started chewing again. He's crazy, I thought. Red made him crazy.

As quickly as the eel had attacked the *ulua* flesh, Uncle Raz jammed the steel hook under its jawbone and backpedaled away as fast as he could.

The instant of puncture brought chaos. Bits of *ulua* drifted away from the writhing, slashing, shaking head. Uncle Raz retreated, running the fishing line through his fingers as he rose to the surface, keeping it taut, pulling the hook deeper into the eel's jaw.

Back on the boat he wound all the slack line around an empty Coke bottle, and pulled back, increasing the pressure on the eel. "He's trying to squirm deeper into his cave," he said. "Get me the gloves."

He told me to hold the bottle while he put the gloves on. "Okay," he said. "Give me a grip."

I wrapped some line around his left hand. Then, reaching down over the transom, Uncle Raz took one turn of line around his other hand and leaned backward, pulling with the strength of his back and pressing upward with his legs. The evaporating salt water on his back beaded up and glinted sunlight against his red-brown skin. For the moment I'd forgotten about chopping away the black coral, absorbed in the small war Uncle Raz had started with the moray. There was no way, I thought, that the eel was going to beat this man.

"Put your hand on the line," he said. I touched it with my fingertips and could feel the eel thrashing on the other end. Red stood behind us with his arms crossed.

"Just his head," Uncle Raz said. "Most of him is still in the cave. The buggers are strong."

We waited an hour while Uncle Raz fought with the eel. And though the thrashing had long since stopped, the eel solidly resisted with occasional tugging outbursts. A splotch of blood soaked through the bandage on Uncle Raz's arm. It was swelling and must have ached, but he ignored it.

Honey watched us for a while, then silently slipped into the ocean to cool off. She climbed aboard less than a minute later. The water-filled top of her two-piece swimsuit slipped down an inch as she climbed over the transom. Red stood next to Uncle Raz with a beer in his hand, scowling at the time we were wasting.

Finally, when the sun was halfway from its peak to the horizon, Uncle Raz gained an inch of line. It woke me from the boredom of waiting, like a singing reel puts the life back into you after long hours trolling for marlin.

"Hah! Now you feel the pain!" Uncle Raz said, fixing his eyes on the line. "We got him now, Red. We *got* him!"

Uncle Raz's hands must have been cramping pretty badly, because he kept removing them from the line, one at a time, and opening and closing his fist. One inch gained in an hour didn't seem to me like much to get so optimistic about.

When another two inches of reluctant line came out of the ocean, Uncle Raz almost giggled. Then, as if the line had been cut, he found himself falling backward, stumbling into the fighting chair.

"He's out!"

Uncle Raz got back up and took in more line in long, steady pulls, as if he were hypnotized. Red and I, and even Honey, peered over the transom, and from the depths could see the shimmering brown snakelike image rising to the surface.

Uncle Raz let the eel pace back and forth along the back of

the boat until it lulled itself into a sense of safety, until it felt no reason to panic.

"Sonny! The club!" he said, and I handed him the heavy, gray wooden fish mallet. He held it still in one hand, waiting for the right moment. Uncle Raz lifted the line and slowly pulled the eel from the water.

At the precise moment the brain crossed the sharp edge of the gunwale, he beat down on it, over and over, until the eel stopped thrashing. Honey covered her ears with her hands.

When the eel was dead Uncle Raz pulled it into the stern cockpit. "Holey moley!" Six feet of muscle and slimy mucus, nearly as thick as Uncle Raz's arm.

Even though Uncle Raz was pretty sure it was dead, he kept his feet as far from the eel as he could, and told Red and me to stay back.

But the eel was as lifeless as a hose, almost pitiful. Uncle Raz put it in the fish box.

With the eel gone and the way to the bottom of the hollow clear, Uncle Raz returned for the black coral. Red and I followed him again and looked into the cavern. Everything was calm, as if no battle had ever occurred. The black coral was framed below by the sides of the well.

Within seconds Uncle Raz had removed it from its base without losing a single point on its thousand branches. He rose slowly, delicately carrying the black jewel.

Red ran out of air and rose to the surface, but Uncle Raz and I paused to look back down. Where the black coral had been there was only a small, empty white sand oval. It must have lived there a hundred years. We'd scared the rainbow of fish into the caverns. The well was a bland pit, silent.

Red beat us to the boat and climbed aboard. Uncle Raz carefully handed him the black coral and pulled himself up after it, then reached over the gunwale to give me a hand.

The coral sparkled in the sun. Its branches reached out in every direction, growing more delicate toward the ends, like a leafless tree of obsidian. It nearly filled a third of the stern cockpit. Honey sat up and pulled her knees to her chin.

"Honey," Red said. "It ain't no marlin, but it's something."

"What is it?" she asked from behind her reflecting sunglasses.

"Black coral. A beaut, ain't it?"

"Yes, it is," Honey whispered.

"It'll look great behind the bar," Red said.

Honey took off her glasses and looked up at him. Her eyes were so beautiful I could feel it in my stomach, a kind of tingling. She smiled at Red, and he beamed over at Uncle Raz. Just before Honey put her glasses back on she glanced at me, eye to eye, as if she could read my thoughts.

"Sonny," Uncle Raz commanded. "Put the gear away and throw some water over the deck.".

The sun was low to the horizon by then and the sky was beginning to close down. As excited as Uncle Raz had been about getting the coral for Red, he was strangely silent on the way back to the harbor. I gazed at the trees and coves and scattered houses along the shoreline as we cruised by. The land rose from black lava washed by white foam, through lush green jungle midlands and on up Hualalai, past the tree line to its purple peak, a huge, magnificent mountain that never failed to free my imagination.

But this time it wasn't the same. I was staring at the island but my mind was miles away. I felt edgy, thinking about the dream-memories that still surfaced, the same words that kept coming back to me whenever something scared me. *Don't ever do that again, boy! Never!* I'd heard them somewhere. But where? I felt empty not knowing. I wondered if Uncle Raz was feeling empty, too, thinking about the pit where the black coral had been. The fish would return, but the well would never look the same again.

Just before we reached the harbor, we passed by the point where the Hilton was going to be. When Uncle Raz caught me watching him staring at the point, he looked away and took us quickly into the harbor.

Red paid Uncle Raz a hundred dollars more than he had to, and tipped me with a twenty dollar bill, the biggest tip I'd gotten that summer. I couldn't believe it—twenty dollars! A brand new spinning rig came immediately to mind, and maybe a fishing tackle box if there was any money left over. I thanked Red again and again, and shook his hand.

He smiled and patted me on the back. "Lots more where that came from, boy."

Uncle Raz pulled the stern up next to the pier and followed Red off the boat. I handed Honey's bag up to Uncle Raz.

Honey put her hand out for me to help her up onto the pier. She paused a moment, holding my hand and taking off her glasses with her other hand. She smiled, then leaned close and kissed my forehead.

Uncle Raz drove Red and Honey off to Kona Inn with the black coral nestled safely into the center of an old truck tire in the bed of the truck.

I dragged the hose out of the stern storage hatch and screwed it into the fresh-water spigot on the pier. Water shot out into the harbor when I turned it on, making bright slapping sounds. I stood barefoot on the warm concrete watching Uncle Raz's truck drive through the village until it was swallowed up by the trees at the end of the seawall.

"Hey!" a man yelled. "No waste the water. Turn 'um off if you're not going to use it."

"Sorry," I said, snapping back. I started washing down the boat, feeling richer than I'd been in a long time.

When Uncle Raz returned, we took the boat out to its mooring without saying much to each other. He moved his arm tenderly, as if it were hurting pretty badly. Just before climbing into the skiff to come back to shore, Uncle Raz said, "We made a lot of money this time, Sonny."

I nodded and said, "Yeah."

Uncle Raz started the outboard and swung around toward the pier. The sky had turned red out near the horizon, and a rich, deep metal-blue above the mountain.

The skiff vibrated through me as I leaned over the side, studying the dark, mysterious coral heads and bright turquoise sandy spots as we glided over them. I traced a small circle on my forehead with my fingertips, tranquilized by the hum of the outboard. It was strange, but I missed Honey.

I met Uncle Raz on the pier at six-thirty the next morning to get the boat ready for an eight-o'clock charter. He parked his truck crooked in the parking stall and sat there a minute before getting out. He looked as if he'd just gotten up, a flattened swirl of hair mashed on the side of his head.

When we took the skiff out to get the *Optimystic*, I noticed that his arm wasn't bandaged. The area around the eel bite was red and swollen, but it didn't seem to bother him.

Then, when we brought the boat in from the mooring, he banged the hull into the truck-tire fenders alongside the pier, leaving a jagged black scar on the side of the boat.

Dad was gassing up the *Ipo* at the time and had seen the whole thing. He came over and dropped down onto the *Optimystic* to see what was going on.

"Nothing," Uncle Raz said. "I just have a sore arm, that's all."

Dad took one look at the bite and headed straight for Uncle

Raz's ship-to-shore radio to call Uncle Harley. He told him to get on down and take Uncle Raz to the doctor. The bite was infected. He needed some attention, and probably a tetanus shot.

But it wasn't Uncle Harley who showed up. It was Tutu Max.

"Shee, you need to get married," she said, studying Uncle Raz's arm. "You need someone to act as your brain. How come you let this get so bad?"

Uncle Raz groaned. "Wha'choo doing here, old lady?"

Tutu Max ignored the question and shook her head. "I getting too old for this. Look at you, all puff up on the arm and you don't even know it."

Uncle Raz frowned, and Tutu Max wagged a finger at him.

"Get in the car. We going to the doctor."

"But . . ."

"No buts. Get!"

"Don't worry," Dad said, trying to suppress a smile. "Sonny and I will take care of the charter."

Tutu Max not only carted Uncle Raz up to the doctor, but also took him back to her house and kept him there for two days, and she wouldn't even let him drink a beer. Dad and Uncle Harley thought it was hilarious.

I carried the twenty dollar bill around for more than a week. I could feel it in my front pocket, folded once and lying flat against my thigh.

Finally I bought a new spinner and a fishing tackle box with three trays, the kind I'd wanted for years. I even had enough left over for a couple of new lures.

I should have been bragging to Keo about my riches. *He'd* never gotten a twenty dollar tip. And as far as I knew, he'd never been kissed by someone as beautiful as Honey.

But I kept it all to myself.

6

You Would Cry to See Waiakea Town
(1960)

Whenever I stood at the edge of the island, where rock and water boomed in a blaze of white brightness, I always chose to face the sea. "Never underestimate its power," Dad had told me. "It could wake, yawn, and swallow you between one heartbeat and the next."

On Saturday, May 21, 1960, I spent the night up at Keo's house. Uncle Harley was visiting Tutu and Grampa Mendoza in Honolulu, and Dad and Uncle Raz had driven over to the other side of the island, to the Suisan fish market in Hilo.

Aunty Pearl sat at the kitchen table listening to the one Honolulu radio station we could get in Kona and looking at some photos in an old album.

The day's heavy overcast had broken up, and in the gaps between clouds, the first stars, like tiny silver fish scales, sparkled against a purple twilight sky.

"Boys, come see these pictures," Aunty Pearl called after we'd finished feeding the dogs. We came in and sat across from her at the table, which was more like a booth at a restaurant. The chairs moved around but the table was nailed to the floor and to the wall just under the window.

"Look at this," she said, shaking her head. "Here's your daddy, Keo, when he was just a little older than you. What a *lolo* that boy was." She turned the album around and there was Uncle Harley waving at the camera with a stick fish in his mouth. It shot out from both sides of his face, about half a foot on each side.

Keo laughed at the picture. "Was he really that crazy?"

"Crazy? That was *normal* for him. He was always showing off for me." She turned the album back around to face her, then smiled, and tapped the picture with her finger. "I never loved anyone but that silly boy there with the fish in his mouth." It was impossible to imagine Uncle Harley without Aunty Pearl.

"Show Sonny the one where he's swimming with the cow," Keo said.

"Gotta go way back for that one." Aunty Pearl flipped the pages to the beginning. "Here it is. There's Daddy by the cow, and there," she said to me, pointing to a boy standing on the sand watching the cowboys swim the cows out to the cattle boat, "is *your* daddy."

Dad and Uncle Harley, like me and Keo.

"And look, there's your Uncle Raz." He was almost out of the photo, down the beach with a stick in his hand. "Your tutu said Raz was always chasing crabs, even when the cowboys came." She clicked her tongue and shook her head. "He never could stand still."

I flipped through the pages and stopped when I found a picture of Dad with his arm around my mother. They must have been about eighteen or nineteen. They were standing on the pier, a sampan behind them, and the palace in the trees beyond. Dad was thinner then, and not as muscular. My mother was about the same height as him, but with much lighter hair, blond mixed with light brown. She was leaning into Dad, her head tilted into his neck and one hand on his chest.

"Crissy was a sweet, sweet girl, Sonny," Aunty Pearl said. "Your daddy still misses her. It's hard even now for him to talk about her."

I felt bad for Dad, but as much as I wanted to I couldn't feel his sadness. My mother was just a name and a few photographs that held no life. She was a part of Aunty Pearl's time, and of Dad's.

Yet the picture of her hand on Dad's chest stayed with me long into the night.

When I awoke the next morning something wasn't right. Keo was asleep on the other side of the room, but other than his light breathing, there were no sounds—no dogs, no birds, no chickens clucking, no nothing—and the small window was full of gray clouds. Keo's electric clock was frozen at 1:05.

When I tapped his shoulder, he woke instantly, and sat up.

"Something's wrong," I said. His eyes were both wild and blank-looking at the same time. Uncle Harley had trained him well. No one in our family ever took more than a few seconds to get out of bed once awakened.

"The clock stopped in the middle of the night, and the sky's dark. Maybe a big storm."

Keo tried the lamp, but it didn't work. He slid out of bed, and I followed him into the dark kitchen. None of the switches worked there either. But strangest of all was the absence of Aunty Pearl. She always got up before us.

After prowling around we found her sitting outside on the porch, listening to a small transistor radio. The voice coming through was weak and covered with static. When she saw us she put her finger to her lips. We sat down on either side of her.

The reception may have been bad but there was no mistaking the news: a series of powerful tidal waves had hit the islands, but the worst had devastated the coastal areas of Hilo.

Dad! There, at the fish market in Waiakea Town—as close to the ocean as you can get.

The reporter sounded excited and a little shook up. "The force of the *big* wave was tremendous," he said. "At least twenty-six bodies have been found." Then, in a way that sent shivers through my scalp, he said, "You would cry to see Waiakea Town . . . not one wall is left."

I jumped to my feet and walked away, and then back, then away again. Aunty Pearl and Keo sat side by side, as if they were thinking of what to say.

Aunty Pearl finally spoke. "Keo, take the Jeep. Go get Grampa."

Keo was only thirteen. Aunty Pearl had never let him drive the Jeep when Uncle Harley wasn't there, even though she knew he could handle it. But we couldn't call Grampa Joe because the phone was out.

"Go through the pastures and stay off the main road," she said.

It took a few minutes to get the Jeep going. But Uncle Harley always parked it on a hill so he could kick-start it when the battery ran down. I pushed, and Keo got it going. We turned uphill and inched and jerked our way through the tangled jungle of Christmas berry and towering mango trees, never shifting out of first gear. The road was rocky and overgrown.

"Did you feel an earthquake last night?" Keo asked over the whine of the engine.

"No. There wasn't one."

"Yeah," Keo said. "It would have got me up, too. There must have been a big one, though. Somewhere."

We lurched from side to side in squeaking seats as the Jeep

climbed higher, from pasture to pasture. Keo sat forward with both hands on the wheel, chin high, trying to see the trail.

Tutu Max filled the doorway when we drove into the yard, as if she'd known we'd be coming. She held the screen door open and didn't say a word about Keo driving. "Grampa's listening to the radio."

He was sitting at the kitchen table.

"Mama wants you," Keo said.

Grampa Joe nodded and went to the back porch for his rubber boots. Everything was still wet from the night.

Tutu Max gave us each a piece of coffee cake and a hug. "Your daddy will be okay," she said, her warm hand on the back of my neck. "They had warnings four hours before the first wave."

Grampa Joe followed us out. Keo hesitated when we got to the Jeep.

"What you waiting for?" Grampa Joe said, waving his hand toward the driver's seat.

For the first time that morning Keo smiled. Grampa Joe kept his irritated, worn-out look and climbed into the shotgun seat. I jumped in behind him and we bounced back down to Keo's house, the engine growling and spitting, and the steering wheel jerking back and forth in Keo's hands as he drove over the rocks.

When we got back to the house, Grampa Joe asked Aunty Pearl if she knew where Dad and Uncle Raz stayed when they went to Hilo. But she didn't. "We better go find 'um," Grampa Joe said. "Could be days before they get the phones back."

"You boys go get your thongs and a blanket," Aunty Pearl said. "I make some sandwiches."

Grampa Joe drove us down to the harbor to see what we could find out before heading over to the other side of the island.

The electricity was out everywhere. On our side of the island the waves had been more like a high tide than tidal waves. In the harbor most of the damage was done on the grounds of the hotels close to the ocean—the King Kam, the Kona Inn, and Waiaka Lodge.

The fishing boats were all at their moorings in the bay, their skippers standing around on the pier talking. Nearby, a hotel crew was picking through a mess of tables and chairs and mopping water out of King Kam Hotel's main lobby.

The radio said that the waves—called *tsunamis*—had been set off by an earthquake in Chile. There were four or five waves, one of them so big that it ran through lower Hilo like a gigantic bulldozer. A lot of people were killed because they didn't believe a wave was coming.

"Let's go," Grampa Joe said, firing up the Jeep.

We drove up Palani Road heading over the top of the island, wind batting at our ears. The sandwiches Aunty Pearl had made for us lay on the seat next to me, but the thought of eating made me feel sick. I wrapped a blanket around me when we rose into the cool, damp air of the uninhabited highlands.

Heavy clouds pushed in on Hilo as we dropped down toward the bay from the mountain. With the traffic signals out cars nudged carefully ahead, strangely silent, no honking. The police and National Guard had the lower section of town completely blocked off. We inched our way closer, glancing at the sullen faces in the cars around us.

Then we saw Mamo Street—now an oozing, muddy pile of rubble. The streets just above it were thick with cars and people caught up in the confusion. We could have *walked* faster than we drove.

Even with the blanket I sat huddled forward in the Jeep hugging myself. But the cold didn't seem to bother Grampa Joe. He was a lot like Dad that way, quiet and kept to himself. Keo didn't seem to care either, his eyes squinting ahead as if trying to find Dad and Uncle Raz somewhere in the mass of stunned people.

Finally Grampa Joe pulled into a field of wet, knee-high grass, and parked under a clump of hao trees. My body tingled when he turned off the engine and the vibrating Jeep sat still. Every sound was muffled as my ears adjusted to the silence.

"We walk from here," Grampa Joe said. Keo and I jumped out. After a couple of hours on the road it felt good to move around.

It was a little past noon, only six or seven hours since the wave had hit. The wave. Every time I thought of it a rush of dread pushed through my stomach. The vision of finding Dad and Uncle Raz dead lurked in my mind. But surely they would have heard the warnings. They would have headed for higher ground.

We were about a half mile from the ocean, inland from the fish market. Grampa Joe led the way. Except for the far-off wail of an occasional police siren, everything was still. Deserted.

When the smell of dead fish and swamp muck hit me I knew we were getting close. At first a thin slick of mud covered the road, then ankle-deep mud and boards with nails in them, and cane trash from the sugar mill miles down the coast.

And clothing.

"I didn't *think* it would be easy," Grampa Joe muttered when he saw the barricade. We'd just rounded a bend in the road. Two guards in army rain gear watched as we approached, then loomed over us with somber faces set back into the hoods of their olive-green ponchos.

"Can't go beyond this point without a pass," one guard said.

"Listen," Grampa Joe said calmly, "we're looking for two men who were in Waiakea last night. We don't know if they're dead or alive."

"If they were anywhere near this place last night they probably had about a fifty-fifty chance," the guard said, sounding as if he'd been there for days. "There was a warning. Go check the intermediate school. They set up an emergency shelter there."

"Where can we get a pass?" Grampa Joe asked.

The guard stared down at him, irritated. "You can go to the Civic Auditorium or the Civil Defense Office."

Grampa Joe nodded and headed back up the way we'd just come. Keo and I followed him back toward the Jeep. I felt slightly dizzy. *Emergency shelter.* Rows of bodies laid out on the ground, covered with blankets.

Suddenly, Grampa Joe angled off into the tall grass along the river. "Take all day to get a pass," he muttered, as we snuck through the trees and skirted the barricade.

I started breathing quickly, sucking in uneven gulps of air. I tried to slow down and breathe normally, but couldn't. I'd never felt that way before, like something awful was going to happen and I was powerless to do anything but keep moving toward it.

The rubble crammed up into the back end of the river was incredible—splintered buildings, boulders, cars, bent and twisted steel beams, dead fish, telephone poles, and cane trash. And a sampan as long as Dad's, red hull to the sky.

Grampa Joe stopped suddenly, staring into the mud on the other side of the river. Keo and I quickly saw what he was looking at—a red truck, a Toyota like Uncle Raz's.

"Lots of people drive red trucks," Grampa Joe said.

Dad would have heard the warnings and made it out of there. But Uncle Raz . . . Could he have gotten antsy and argued that it was a false alarm? Could he have talked Dad into going back into Waiakea Town?

Men were everywhere, with shovels, axes, crowbars, hoes, and ropes, working in heaps of mud and boards. No guards bothered us once we were inside the barricaded area. They were as confused and overwhelmed as we were.

I stood facing the ocean, the mucky world strangely peaceful. I was looking at the mouth of the river . . .

The mouth of the *river*!

The fish market was gone! *Waiakea Town* was gone!

Not damaged, gone—a whole town, flattened and pushed up into the heel of the river, splintered and shoved inland in pieces.

The mouth of the river and the shapes of the hills in the distance stood like unrecognizable landmarks, ghosts of another century. Steel parking meters were bent flat to the sidewalks. Where buildings had once been, there were only vacant cement pads. The houses, shops, and boats lay farther back, in shattered heaps, with men digging through them. Fish trapped in puddled gutters flopped hopelessly in brown, foot-deep ponds.

"No need to go any farther," Grampa Joe finally said. "Better we help, and ask questions."

Nearby, three men were pulling and prying tangled boards apart, trying to get to something beneath them. A woman watched them work, as if in a trance. She stood off to the side with her arms crossed, still as a gravestone.

Grampa Joe went over to help. Keo and I followed, picking our way through the mud. Like fools we'd come to Hilo completely unprepared, in all respects. Nails jutted from splintered boards. Chunks of broken glass and other sharp objects suspended within the mud threatened to slice through the thin rubber thongs on our feet. I searched for something solid to step on. *He's okay.* Dad's okay. He *had* to be.

Keo glanced over at me, his face drawn. I'd never seen him look more somber, as if he'd already given in to the worst, and was now turning to me for a final shred of hope. Then he turned away and continued picking his way through the debris.

Off to my left four cars were smashed into each other, bent

and tangled together, like steel seaweed. I didn't try to figure out what it took to get them that way. Everything I felt in those first few moments came to me in small, manageable scenes. By instinct I moved into a protective matter-of-factness, a way of being that allowed me to accept everything I saw and thought as simply being the way it was. Dad and Uncle Raz were *neither* dead nor alive, they simply were—somewhere. But *where*?

Keo and I and Grampa Joe helped the three men dig through the broken boards. After a while, one of the men stopped and looked up. "We're looking for a girl," he said. "A small girl."

Grampa Joe winced, and studied the muck around his feet.

We pulled damp boards away and piled them off to the side without speaking. But we had to ask questions. Grampa Joe broke the spell slowly, and thoughtfully. Our need for information was as great as their need for silence.

"Did you have warning?" Grampa Joe finally asked.

"Plenty warning."

We continued to pull trash from the pile. Then, minutes later, the man went on. "Four hours, about, between the sirens and the waves. Some people never left. Some came back just before the waves hit, thinking it was a false alarm. We've had them before."

Grampa Joe nodded, then said, "We're looking for two men. They were at the fish market."

The man shook his head, as if to say, "poor souls."

We helped them for about fifteen minutes, then drifted away. The little they'd said, though, gave me hope. Dad had had time to think.

But the red truck in the river . . .

For the next hour we made slow progress through small groups of mud-covered people. Digging. Still finding bodies. As we worked our way back toward the Jeep the three of us broke apart. I felt better alone, as, I suppose, did Keo and

Grampa Joe. In the river I saw three more half-sunken sampans. Whoever owned them should have taken them out and dealt with the waves at sea.

I studied the mud for a safe place to step, pushing slowly down into the muck. I was so worried about getting cut that, at first, I didn't recognize what I was staring at.

I held my breath. Didn't move.

A *foot* . . .

A small, muddy foot.

I stood suspended over it, sluggishly, realization coming slowly. A great, burning ball rose up inside me, a hot wave covering me. My skin rose in the sweat of fear. A small foot. Rising just inches from the mud.

Keo and Grampa Joe had moved on, unaware. It must have been a full minute before I could speak.

"Wait . . . *wait!*"

I knelt down into the mud and started to move the rocks and cane trash and splintered wood from around the foot. Once Aunty Pearl had shielded Keo and me from the squashed body of one of the cats that hung around Keo's house. Now there was no soft voice, no nice way of telling me that the foot belonged to a child, a person younger than me who was dead.

Keo and Grampa Joe hurried back and stood over me. I looked up at them.

"Oh, no . . ." Grampa Joe said quietly, kneeling down at my side.

We scooped away the thickening mud, handful by handful. She lay face down with one leg bent back. As if she were as delicate as rice paper, we dug around her, leaving her as she'd fallen. Finally Grampa Joe lifted her and held her, as he would have held a sleeping child. She was a small, thin girl, about seven years old, wearing pajamas.

"Keo," Grampa Joe said quietly, "go find a policeman."

I thought of the woman staring into the rubble as the three men had searched it. Was this *her* child? The sight of Grampa Joe holding her made my chest feel shallow, and tight, but I wanted to see her, to see what it was like being dead. A quivering sensation began in my ears. *This is how Dad felt when my mother died.* He would have called to her—*Crissy, come back, come back.* Then he'd have realized that she was gone, and known that they were both alone, he in life and she in death. He would have screamed, silently, way down inside himself, pounding his fists against his chest because he'd know that there was absolutely nothing he could do to change what had happened.

"Sonny," Grampa Joe said. I must have looked as if I were about to pass out. With a tenderness I'd never heard before, from anyone, he said, "It's as it should be, boy. The living have no edge over the dead. She doesn't feel your pain."

Keo came back with an army guard and two men. One of them was the man who'd been searching for the child. His eyes watered when he saw the girl. He closed them for a moment, then nodded to the guard.

Grampa Joe held the girl until the man was ready to take her. When he did, he thanked Grampa Joe, bowing his head slightly, then carried her away, the other men following silently. Grampa Joe watched them leave, the front of his shirt covered with mud.

The memory of the small foot, the muddy face and caked hair, the closed eyes, began to consume me. I took in steady gulps of air, trying to settle down, but it only made it worse. More than anything else in the world I needed to stand beside Dad, to have him rest his hand on my shoulder, and to ask him why.

My vision blurred as we made our way back through

the deep grass to the Jeep, a stink rising from the scarred earth.

Just before we got to the grove of trees where the Jeep was parked, Keo, who'd gone on ahead, turned back and started jumping up and down. Grampa Joe had been walking next to me with his hand on my shoulder. He stopped. "Thank God."

Uncle Raz sat alone in the driver's seat of Uncle Harley's Jeep, his arms crossed, asleep. I ran past Keo and shook him awake. "Where's Dad?" I said. "Is he okay?"

Uncle Raz jumped, and grabbed the steering wheel. "Sheese! You want me to have a heart attack? What the hell are you *lolos* doing here, anyway?"

"Looking for you," Keo said.

"You buggers," he said, sounding angry, but clearly pleased to see us. "Don't scare me like that. I was going up to the school when I saw the Jeep in the grass. I thought I was going nuts, it was *Harley's* Jeep! Sonny," he added, looking at me, "your daddy's okay. Don't worry."

"Where is he?"

"Suisan and some people from Tuna Packers wanted to get together with the fishermen. Raymond went while I waited to see who'd show up here. Big problems. No ice to ice fish, the ice plant is gone. And they got to clean out the river so the boats can get back in. At least those that went out in the first place."

Grampa Joe humphed.

Keo told Uncle Raz that we knew about the wave from the transistor. "No phone, no lights, no nothing. We didn't know if you were dead or alive, so we came over."

Uncle Raz got out of the Jeep and put his arms around me and Keo. "Thanks," he said. "We tried to call, too. When the siren started wailing we went up the hill. Half the people just stayed in their houses waiting for another warning or something."

"Did you see the wave?" Keo asked.

"No, but we heard it. There was more than one, but the big one came in with a roaring sound, first like hissing, then rushing louder and louder. Then the whole town went black."

"Where's your truck?" Grampa Joe said.

"Up by the school. Why?"

Grampa Joe glanced over at me and Keo. "Just wondered." For a minute no one spoke.

"Let's go get Raymond," Uncle Raz finally said, climbing back in and starting the Jeep before he'd finished the sentence.

He drove us out of the grass in low gear, the Jeep jerking over uneven ground. The sound of the grinding engine soothed me, even the sickly, familiar smell of its exhaust.

My throat burned as I watched Dad walk out of the school toward us. *Dad*, more a part of me than anyone else on earth.

"Hi, son," he said, as if nothing out of the ordinary had happened. I wanted to hug him, but I didn't, not in front of everyone.

"We were worried," I said.

He put his hand on my shoulder and squeezed.

Dad and Uncle Raz said they were going to stay in Hilo for a few more days to help out. Many people were still missing.

Grampa Joe fired up the Jeep. I climbed into the seat next to him. Keo wanted to sleep in the back.

The old pockmarked saddle road was still damp, but the rain had passed, and patches of clear sky scattered acres of blue into the mist and low clouds of the high country. Dusk was closing in and the air swirling around us in the Jeep was getting cooler.

Just above Waiki'i, Grampa Joe pulled the Jeep off the road. It was dark by then, and cold. Keo was curled up in the backseat under a blanket.

"Want to drive?" Grampa Joe said. "Plenty dark. No police around here. No *anybody* around here."

". . . Sure," I said.

"Get over here then," Grampa Joe said, hitting me in the arm. "Do you some good."

My feet barely reached the floorboard when I stepped on the clutch. The steering wheel pulled in my hands, complaining about every crack and stone on the edge of the road. The warmth of the engine spread around my feet, radiating off the metal.

The clouds finally cleared and a zillion stars filled the blackness around me. I squinted over at Grampa Joe when I reached the stop sign at the junction where the saddle road met Mamalahoa. He was asleep, or just sitting there like Uncle Raz had been, with his arms crossed and his eyes closed.

I sat thinking at the stop sign, the engine idling and nothing in sight except the stars and the beams of light in front of me. I was twelve years old, driving my cousin and my grandfather home on the main road in pitch black; I'd seen a dead girl; I'd thought my father was dead. Somehow being behind the wheel felt right, as if I could control something in my life, if only for an hour or so. The soothing vibration of the Jeep pushing through the night, and the open spaces, on all sides and above me, endlessly into the stars, seemed to have the power to lift the weight I felt inside. Maybe that's why Dad was a fisherman. Maybe that's why he spent so much time alone.

I drove around Mauna Loa, across the island highlands, and all the way to Grampa Joe's doorstep before he opened his eyes.

His face was white in the reflected glow of the headlights. He got out slowly, yawning and rubbing the stubble on his jaw, playing the part of an old man. "You okay, Omilu?" he asked.

"I'm okay, Grampa."

He went into the house and closed the door without looking back.

I drove down into the thick, black coffee grove as Keo climbed into the front seat, keeping the blanket around him.

Grampa Joe had called me Omilu, a term he used sparingly, and it meant a lot to me to be compared to the *ulua*, a fish that would give any man a tough, two-fisted battle.

I drove Keo home to Aunty Pearl, and watched as his mother took him in and gave him a long, surrounding hug. The blanket still covered him, half of it hanging down the porch steps. Then Aunty Pearl smiled and pulled me into her arms next to Keo.

Someday Dad would tell me. I would make him tell me. To him, and to Aunty Pearl, my mother was Crissy with her hand on Dad's chest, not just an old photograph in a picture album. Once she was as alive as my jumping heart.

Who was she? I would *make* him tell me.

7

Uncharted Waters 's

(1961)

Dad's sampan rolled gently in the low swells as it idled alongside the pier at five in the morning. The black sky held only the faintest hint of sunrise, a light sketch of midnight-blue behind the mountain. Keo and I sat on the stern transom watching Dad and Uncle Harley stow their gear.

Dad glanced over at me. "You can still change your mind and come along, Sonny."

"No, that's okay. I'll stay and keep Keo company."

Dad nodded and went forward to the hold.

Keo scowled at the deck, his arms crossed. Missing a chance to go on an overnight fishing trip to South Point was about as low as it got for Keo. And all because a *girl* was coming to visit.

Uncle Harley put a couple of cases of soda pop and beer into the ice chest. "Don't look so miserable," he said, glancing over to Keo. "Raz will be around if you need anything. You can come along next time. Of course, South Point could be hot this trip, could catch forty or fifty *ono*, never can tell." Uncle Harley smiled, but Keo didn't think it was so funny.

"Let's go," Dad said. "It's gonna be a dynamite day. I can feel it in my bones. Eh, Keo, you didn't hide any bananas on board did you?" Bananas were bad luck of the worst kind.

Keo smiled at that. "Maybe I did."

"Scoot, you two rats," Uncle Harley said. "Throw the lines."

Keo and I pulled the stern closer to the pier and climbed up the truck tires, then untied the boat and tossed the lines down onto the deck. Dad pulled the *Ipo* away and headed out into the dark harbor, the old diesel *tokking* smoothly. Uncle Harley stood in the dim deck light looking back at us, curling the sternline into neat loops in his hand.

Within minutes the *Ipo* was nothing more than a small yellow light shrinking south.

It was quiet in the harbor, and cool. As much as Keo loved being on a boat, I loved being on the pier that early in the morning, a time when Kailua-Kona stood still, with only the anticipation of the day to come rustling around in the air.

But Aunty Pearl had plans for us. Keo and I began the long walk back up the hill to his house.

"Tutu going bring Melanie up here from the airport," Aunty Pearl said. "I want you boys to show her Kailua. This is her first time on the Big Island."

Keo stared out the window. We sat at the kitchen table waiting for the arrival of Melanie McNeil, Keo's mysterious Honolulu cousin. Neither of us had ever met her before. In fact Aunty Pearl had only seen her once many years ago. But, of course, since Melanie's mother was her cousin, Aunty Pearl knew everything there was to know about her. She sounded pretty flashy to me—her *baole* father owned a radio station; her mother was a dancer at the Moana Hotel in Waikiki; she went to private school; and to top it off she was fifteen, a year older than Keo, and two older than me. "Her mother says she can sing like an angel at sunset," Aunty Pearl said. "She has a very, very rare gift."

I wondered what a rich, half-Hawaiian, fifteen-year-old girl who went to private school and could sing like an angel was like. What were we going to show her, anyway? How to fish? How to clean boats? How to shoot BB guns at the dump?

"This is going to be great," Keo said flatly when Aunty Pearl had gone out on the porch to see if anyone was coming up the driveway. "Poor little thing. A whole *week* without her mommy and daddy. Probably never even been away from home before."

"Keo, Sonny, they're here," Aunty Pearl called. Keo looked like he wanted to spit.

We went out just as Tutu Max and Grampa Joe pulled up to the house in a cloud of dust. The door on the driver's side flew open and Tutu Max pushed herself up out of the car.

Grampa Joe got out and opened the back door, just like at a hotel. When Melanie McNeil stepped out into the sun I nearly went speechless.

She looked more like a woman than a girl, dressed up like she was going to church or to dinner at Kona Inn. She was about as tall as me and twice as beautiful as any girl I'd ever seen in my life—dark, silky skin, and eyes as clear as a freshwater pond.

"Aunty Pearl?" Melanie said, looking up to the porch.

"Oh, little baby, you are so *grown up*!" Aunty Pearl said, truly surprised.

Melanie smiled and walked up to hug her like she owned the place.

"This is your cousin, Keo, and his cousin on his father's side, Sonny."

Melanie looked at us in a funny way, as if we were children or the yardmen. "Hi."

Aunty Pearl and Tutu Max gathered Melanie up and shooed her into the house. Grampa Joe came up behind them carrying all four of her suitcases.

After she said good-bye to Tutu Max and Grampa Joe, Melanie followed Aunty Pearl into her room, Keo's room, and closed the door. Aunty Pearl stayed there with her. We could hear Melanie crying, and Aunty Pearl soothing her. Neither of us could make out what she was saying.

We had to wait on the porch. "Don't you go anywhere," Aunty Pearl said to Keo. "She's just tired from her trip."

"Big trip," he said when Aunty Pearl went back inside. "One hour on an airplane."

"I'd cry if I had to stay in your room for a week, too," I said. Keo flicked his fist over and punched me.

"Okay, okay! But you gotta admit, she's darn good-looking, and way too fancy for anything *we* got going," I told him, rubbing my arm.

Keo stared out into the dusty yard. It was so quiet you could hear the flies buzz.

"I don't know if I can last a week of baby-sitting *her*," Keo said. "That'll be about as much fun as scraping barnacles off a boat."

A soft, female voice came from the doorway behind us, like a sudden breeze. "Oh?"

Keo leaped to his feet and turned to face Melanie. "I . . . I mean . . ."

"That's okay, kid," she said. Keo frowned.

She'd changed into a long blue muumuu that looked like it had just come from the store. Her face was flawless—green eyes under sharp eyebrows, and thick brown hair that fanned out over her shoulders. But all Keo saw was the look in her eye.

It said, "Don't get in my way, buster, if you want to live to see tomorrow."

Keo whirled around and stomped over toward the pigpen. I got up and said, "Excuse us," and followed him.

As I walked away I heard her whisper, "*Morons.*"

Keo spent the night down at my house. He told Aunty Pearl I had to feed the dogs and keep an eye on things while Dad was away, and we might just as well stay there for the night. At first she resisted, but caved in when Melanie came through for us and said, "Let the boys have their slumber party, Aunty Pearl. That's okay."

"Now listen, boys," Aunty Pearl said the next morning. "Take Melanie down to see Kona Inn and let her walk through the shops in Kailua. Here's some money to buy lunch for the three of you."

She held a five-dollar bill out, but Keo hesitated.

Melanie grabbed it and stuffed it into a large canvas shoulder bag. "I'll keep that, Aunty Pearl. He'll probably just lose it."

Melanie wore a bright new yellow dress and white leather sandals, and sunglasses. I felt almost naked standing there barefoot in a pair of shorts and a T-shirt.

Keo was steaming. Aunty Pearl pushed him toward the door. He shrugged her hands away and took off down the long, rock and dirt driveway to Hualalai Road without turning to see if Melanie was following.

"Uh . . . you ever been to Kona before?" I asked.

Melanie narrowed her eyes and glared at me, then followed Keo down the driveway without answering, the large bag bouncing off her hip.

I looked up at Aunty Pearl. She shook her head and said in a sighing tone of voice, "I don't know, Sonny, I really don't know."

The three of us marched silently down toward Kailua in single file until Keo stopped a little ways up from town. "I got something to show you," he said looking at Melanie, "that is, if you don't mind getting your feet a little dusty."

She let the bag drop from her shoulder and looked Keo in the eye. "Kid, there's no place on this planet that you could dream of going that I couldn't go as well."

Keo's eyes pinched down when she said *kid*.

"Follow me, *Queenie*," he said.

They stared at each other with machete looks.

Keo bolted off into the dry grass and scrub-tree jungle alongside the road, bending low to squeeze through the middle strands of a barbed-wire fence that separated the road from a tangled cow pasture. The grass was mashed down between the trees so I knew there were cows around, and maybe bulls.

Melanie pulled her dress up high, halfway up her thighs, and bent through the fencing. I followed, watching out for thorns and bulls.

She kept pace with Keo, stride for stride, both of them moving through the trees much faster than necessary. We climbed over old stone walls covered with brush and vines, walls built hundreds of years earlier by the old Hawaiians, and picked our way over outcroppings of sculptured black lava rock frozen in shapes of oozing mud.

Keo stopped when we came to a low depression in the ground, like a dry pond the size of a small, empty swimming pool. A pile of flat stones lay in a small heap in the bottom. Keo called me down into the sink and I helped him lift them away, revealing the entrance to the old lava tube that Uncle Harley had shown us years before. It was one of only two or three places where the underground tunnel came to the surface. Uncle Harley had told us that you could go from near the top of the mountain clear down to the ocean inside the tube, and pop out under water somewhere off Kailua Bay. But I'd never heard of anyone who'd done it.

"Lava tube," Keo said, smirking. "Too bad you can't go in and take a look around."

"Think again, kid. Turn around and don't look until I tell you."

Keo glanced at me.

Tempting as it was, neither of us turned around until she gave us the word. When we did, she was standing there in a blue T-shirt and jeans, barefoot. An inch of yellow dress poked out of the top of her bag. "So what's holding you up?"

"Well . . ." Keo stumbled a minute. "We can't go in very far without a light. Watch out for spider webs and centipedes."

Melanie set her bag down and gave Keo and me a look that said, "So move it."

Keo lowered himself into the hole in the ground, and I *knew* it must have bothered him to do so without first sticking his head down into the opening and flashing a light around to see what was there.

Melanie brushed by me to follow Keo into the hole. The faint smell of soap lingered for a second or two after she passed. Her hair shone in the sunlight. She grabbed it and curled it around as she dropped into the pit.

I followed, as close as I dared. The tube went downhill for only a few feet before the light from the opening nearly disappeared.

"Can't go any farther without a light," Keo said. "Besides, there are so many offshoots you could get lost in here and never get out. One boy went into a lava tube down near Kau, and never came out again." The thought of dying alone in utter blackness made me cringe.

"There are bones in here, too," I added. "I think this was used as a burial cave."

Melanie wasn't impressed. "Let's go deeper. Just till there's no light at all. I want to see pure blackness."

"Not smart," Keo said, passing Melanie and me, and crawling back to the mouth of the tube. "Too easy to get lost."

"What? You *afraid*?"

"No, just smart."

I agreed with Keo, though I liked Melanie's idea. When we'd been in before we had flashlights and hadn't thought to turn them off. It would be something to see.

"How about you?" Melanie said to me.

"Keo's right, it's not a good idea." How could I *not* take Keo's side?

"What a bunch of panties," she said.

Neither of us said another word to her until we got down to Kona Inn, and then only because we had to. Keo strode out ahead of us, leaving me alone with her.

She didn't show any particular interest in Kona Inn, or Kakina's, or even Emma's Store with its freezer full of fudge bars, but she perked up when we ended up down at the harbor.

The *Optimystic* rocked easily alongside the pier, with Uncle Raz sitting in the sun in the fighting chair stripping old line off one of his big reels. It was a hot, full, blue-sky day, and the water sparkled, diamonds glinting on green and blue.

"So," Uncle Raz said when we pulled the stern in and stepped aboard, "you must be Camille's girl."

Melanie gave him a sugary-sweet smile.

"Make yourself at home," Uncle Raz went on, meaning Melanie. Keo and I sat on the stern transom and watched him work while Melanie went into the cabin, then down into the forward hold for a look around.

"You got a nice-looking cousin there, Keo," Uncle Raz said.

"Nice rotten cousin, you mean."

"I don't think she likes us very much," I added.

Uncle Raz laughed without looking up from the reel, the line piling up in a heap at his feet. There must have been a half mile of it.

"You wouldn't want to take her for a boat ride, would you?" Keo asked. What a brilliant idea, I thought. *Very* good.

"Don't you boys get enough boat rides?" Uncle Raz said.

"Not us, Uncle. Her." Keo pointed his chin toward the cabin.

Uncle Raz glanced up at Keo, then back down at the reel and started chuckling and shaking his head. "Too much for you, eh?"

Keo sat there with his arms crossed over his chest.

Melanie was gone about five minutes, then came back out into the sun smiling as if something was going on that only she knew about. She bent down and grabbed a handful of the old fishing line on the deck. "Can I have this?" she asked. Uncle Raz gave her a sure-but-what-the-heck-for look and said, "It's yours, take 'um."

After Uncle Raz had stripped all the line off the reel, Melanie took the pile up on the pier and spread it out. Then holding one end in her hand, she began looping the line around her elbow, like a man or a boy would do, not a girl.

Keo finally looked up. When Melanie had the entire mass of line neatly looped around her hand and elbow, she tied it off in the middle and folded it into her bag, which was beginning to seem like it had no bottom.

"Hey," she said to Keo and me. "Let's go."

Even Uncle Raz looked up at her.

"You follow *me* this time," she said.

Keo rolled his eyes, and Uncle Raz patted his shoulder. "Go on, boys," he said, looking as if he were having a great time. He took the dock line from the stern cleat and pulled the boat closer to the truck tires. Keo and I climbed up onto the pier. I could tell that we were going to hear this story from Uncle Raz again and again.

When we got to the beginning of the seawall, Melanie stopped and turned to us. "This is boring, but I have an idea." She looked at us with wide eyes, waiting for one of us to say, "Yeah? What is it?" But neither of us did.

Melanie frowned at our lack of enthusiasm. "Okay," she said, "I'll go back into the cave myself."

Keo perked up. "It's not a cave, it's a lava tube, and it has a thousand branches inside it. And what do you want to go back *there* for anyway?"

"I want to go way in, where it's dark."

"That's dumb, just dumb," Keo said.

"Anyway, we already did that," I added.

"Okay," she said, "okay. You panties stay here, but that's what *I'm* going to do." She spun around and started walking toward the palace, right down the middle of the road. Then she turned, and walking backward, yelled, "Pantie, pantie, pantie!"

Keo yelled back, "Queenie, queenie, queenie!"

She stared, as if surprised. Keo glared back. Then Melanie turned and stormed away, canvas bag bouncing.

Keo picked up a rock on the side of the road and threw it out into the harbor, and to show that I wasn't going to take it either, I threw one myself. Even so I couldn't help sneaking a peek down toward the palace to see how far she'd gone.

"Your mom's not going to like it if we don't keep an eye on her," I said.

"Let's go down to White Sands and go swimming."

"Okay, but I hate to think of what would happen if she really does go into the lava tube, and gets lost."

We started to walk toward White Sands Beach, the same way Melanie had gone. The beach was a long way down the coast and normally we would have tried to hitch a ride. But Melanie had us all tied up. And I was beginning to think she knew it.

"We can't let her go in there alone," I said, grabbing Keo's arm when we reached the intersection.

"Why not? She doesn't need us. We could be down at South Point catching *ono* by the hundreds right now if it wasn't for her. Anyway, she called us panties."

"Yeah, that's true. But . . ."

Keo stuck his thumb out at the first car to come by, and it stopped. He got in, and when he saw that I wasn't coming with him, he slammed the door. "She's not pulling *me* around by the nose," he said, hanging out the window as the car drove away.

The sun was high, and the pavement was hot. When there were no cars around, I hurried up the middle of the road on the broken white line, which was cooler than the blacktop.

When I finally caught up with Melanie, she just kept on going in silence. The road began to twist and climb up toward the mountain, and the trees and grasses pushed out over the edges of the blacktop. She passed the trail into the lava tube without seeing it.

"That was the trail," I said.

She stopped and looked at me for the first time since I'd caught up with her, then she peeked around me.

"Where is he?" she asked.

"Went to the beach."

"Good."

I glanced down the road, then back at Melanie. "He's not as bad as he seems," I said. "He's just mad about not getting to go fishing with Uncle Harley. Aunty Pearl made him stay home because you were coming."

She stared straight at me and I had to look back down the

road again. "I didn't know that," she said. "Want to come with me?"

I shrugged and said, "Sure."

I followed her into the trees wondering what Keo was doing just then—and what he was going to say the next time I saw him.

What a crazy day. All morning this girl had treated us like small *petoots*, and here I was following her around in the jungle, and *liking* it.

Melanie surprised me by the way she climbed down into the hole in the ground, as if she were getting into a car, she was so fearless. I followed her, nervously groping around in the dark, hoping I wouldn't grab a bat or something else that moved. Soon we sat facing each other in an open area around the first bend in the lava tube. It was about as far as we could go before complete blackness.

"Let's go farther in," she whispered.

I couldn't see her face, only the faintest outline of her head. "Melanie, what Keo said was true."

"Shhh," she said, touching my arm.

I shut up and listened, thinking she'd heard something. Then a light went on.

"Where'd you get *that*?" I asked.

Melanie held a flashlight under her chin, shooting the light upward, making grim shadows over her face.

"Off the boat. And then there's this." She held out the neatly looped and bundled fishing line that she'd gotten from Uncle Raz. "Now we can go into pure darkness."

She crawled back out into the light around the bend and motioned for me to follow. She tied one end of the fishing line to a large rock, working quickly. "What do you think?" she asked.

It wasn't the best knot I'd seen, but it would do. Melanie smiled, then said, "Ready?"

"I guess so."

The tube narrowed and twisted and turned off at sharp angles and opened into big areas, only to shrink again into nearly impassable slits. And like the branches of a tree it shot off into side alleys or completely new mile-long tunnels for all I could tell. At one point we had to get down on our stomachs and squeeze through to go any farther. On the other side was a large, round room. Water dripped from one wall and fell into a small mud hole. The air was cold, and the room smelled like a rusty Jeep in a junk pile after a rain.

"This should be far enough," she said, so low I could barely hear her. It was one time I agreed with her completely. We sat next to each other and leaned against the dry side of the room.

Then Melanie turned the flashlight off.

Neither of us moved. I held my breath in honor, I suppose, of the complete and utter lack of light, so profound, so foreign. I couldn't believe that my eyes were wide open and finding it absolutely impossible to focus on anything at all. Something would appear, I thought, as my eyes adjusted. But everything remained completely black. And if it weren't for the dripping water, the silence would have been every bit as piercing as the darkness.

"Wow," Melanie whispered. "Wow, wow, wow, wow, wow."

We sat without speaking for a long time, listening to the drip. A voice kept chattering on somewhere inside my mind, rushing in to fill the empty spaces, not knowing what to do with this new state of being.

Then, as if floating down from a heavy mist that filtered through tall eucalyptus trees on the high midlands of Maùna Kea, I heard what was without question the most beautiful sound I'd ever thought possible to hear.

A voice. Clear, crisp, gentle. Perfect.

"*Pupu, binubinu, pupu, binubinu e . . .*"

When Aunty Pearl had told Keo and me that Melanie McNeil could sing like an angel it had passed over me in less time than I spent thinking about the dirt under my fingernails. But now that voice was inside me, moving outward, soothing my uneasiness about being in the blackness, and igniting feelings I never knew I had.

For a time my own inner voice stopped its yakking, and listened.

". . . *o ke kaba kai . . .*"

I sat perfectly still, as if the slightest movement would cause her to stop. The sound of her voice drenched me in heat, fanning a growing fire in my chest, and sending strange tingling sensations wisping down my arms. I saw myself on a breathless sea in uncharted waters, standing at the rail of an old schooner, waiting for a sign, waiting for something to happen. Then I was underwater, gagging. *Don't you ever do that again . . .* I put my hands over my ears as if to silence the awful, unexplainable dream-memory. What *was* it? I almost said something to Melanie, but didn't.

". . . *pupu, binubinu e . . .*"

When she stopped, and all was silent again, I willed the voice to return, trying to absorb the sound, knowing this was a moment I'd never forget. The wrenching dream-memory left me shaking. I wanted to be closer to Melanie, to have her sing again, to calm me down.

Then I heard her crying, softly.

"Melanie? What's wrong?"

I waited, listening to the dripping water while her trembling slowed.

"Daddy's sick. He almost died. He's in the hospital with pneumonia." She was silent a moment, then went on. "My mother sent me here so she could be with him." She started crying again. "What if he dies?"

"Yeah," I said, barely whispering.

That's what she was crying about in Keo's room.

The heavy blackness of the lava tube closed in on me. *What if he died?*

What if *my* Dad died? My tongue felt dry, remembering Waiakea Town.

I fumbled around on the ground with my hand until I found Melanie. I traced her position. She was sitting with her knees up and her arms folded across her chest. She reached for my hand when I touched her. The palm of her hand, where it met with mine, was damp. I felt it trembling. I could feel her wiping her eyes with her free hand. We sat in silence a long time. I wanted to tell her that my mother had died. But I didn't.

"Let's get out of here," Melanie finally said.

She turned on the flashlight and every drifting thought disappeared. The presence of light alone changed everything—the song, the feelings, the fears. Gone. As if they'd never been there.

We followed the fishing line, crawling back out into the crushing light of day, then walked back through the trees without speaking. Melanie followed a few steps behind me, her bare feet as sure and as tough as mine. I thought about her parents, and about being alone.

"Hey," I said, "I want to show you something."

She let me lead her away from the trail. I veered south through an overgrown jungle of grass and trees, over ancient rock walls and under giant, hard, and brittle kiawe groves. My shirt dampened in the heat and stuck to my back and chest, turning the dust from the cave dark brown.

On a small rise I found what I'd wanted to show her—the

old rock foundation of the first missionary house built on the island of Hawaii, now abandoned for more than a century.

"This must have been the living room," I said half jokingly as we stood on a flat area that seemed to have the best view of the landscape. "A young man and woman, not much older than us, lived here more than a hundred years ago. Built the house themselves, around 1820. It took them six months just to get here to the islands. They left everyone they knew behind and didn't know a soul when they climbed off the boat. *That's* alone."

Aunty Pearl had told me about the old homestead, and Keo and I went looking for it one day. The first time I'd walked through the ruins I was amazed that two young people from Massachusetts had actually sailed away from their home to a place and culture they knew nothing about. After discovering this place I spent hours on the rocks in front of my house, staring out at the ocean and wondering what was out there beyond the far horizon.

Melanie picked something out of the dirt, a chip from a blue and white plate. She cleaned it off and showed it to me. "I wonder if this was from one of their plates."

"Probably was. No one else has lived here."

She smiled at me and put the chip in her bag. "I'm going to keep this to remember *you* by. Come on, let's go back up to Aunty Pearl's."

On the way out to the road she reached over and took my hand, in daylight. The feel of her skin touching mine wasn't at all the same as when Dad put his hand on my shoulder, or when Keo and I would shake to seal a bet. There was some kind of invisible fluid that flowed out of Melanie, then raced through me like lightning, and inhabited my entire body. Is this what girls do? Melt down a boy's body and soul? It didn't matter that she probably only took my hand because she was worried about her father. For the next few minutes even the bulls in the pasture couldn't have taken my attention away from Melanie McNeil.

By the time we left Hualalai Road and headed up the old dirt driveway to Keo's house, a long rain line cut the landscape a mile or so farther up.

When we turned the bend in the road and Keo's house came into view, the dogs started barking and running toward us. Aunty Pearl was going to have a pigpen full of questions when she found out Keo wasn't with us.

"We can't go up there yet," I said, holding Melanie back. "We have to wait for Keo."

Melanie frowned. "Why?"

"Aunty Pearl's going to want to know why he's not with us, and if we tell her he went to the beach instead of staying with you he's going to get into a heap of trouble."

"Ah," she said. "Yes . . ."

Bullet and Blossom came running up, wagging their tails and sniffing around Melanie. I turned and pulled her back down the road. "We can wait for him at the bottom of the driveway, under the mango tree."

"Hooie!" Aunty Pearl called from the porch, waving down to us.

"*Dang*," I muttered. "Now we're in for some explaining."

Aunty Pearl scowled at me when I told her that Keo and I had somehow gotten separated, then she ushered Melanie into the house as if she'd been lost at sea for a week.

Keo came walking up the dusty driveway an hour and a half later. Melanie was sitting next to me on the porch telling me about Honolulu. I'd almost forgotten Keo, I was so absorbed in the sound of her voice so close to my ear and in the warmth coming off her arm less than an inch from mine.

Keo stared at the ground as he came up toward us, as if he were in deep thought over something. And he didn't look too fired-up about seeing the two of us. In fact he stormed on by without a word, as if we weren't even there.

Aunty Pearl's voice rang through the house and out onto the porch. Keo must have whispered back, or said nothing at all, it was so quiet after Aunty Pearl had her say.

Then a door slammed.

"I'm going in and explain to Keo what happened."

"Maybe you'd better leave him alone and let him cool off," Melanie said. But I couldn't sit still.

I knocked once and opened the door to Keo's room. He was lying on his bed with his hands behind his head, staring at the ceiling.

"What do *you* want?" he said when I'd closed the door.

"We were going to wait for you but didn't think about it until it was too late."

"Yeah, sure you were."

"Listen, it's true. Melanie and I were . . ."

"Why don't you just buzz off," he said.

"What . . . ?"

"I said buzz off, beat it, go home already." He sat up with a snap and glared at me.

"Hey," I said. "What are you getting so bent about, it was *you* who left."

"And now it's time for *you* to leave!" he said, standing up. "First I can't go fishing because I have to baby-sit, then you take off and get me in trouble, and now I gotta stay home tomorrow . . . all because of you and that stuck-up queen out there!" Keo pushed me as he talked.

"Now wait a minute," I said, ignoring the push. "Melanie . . ."

"Melanie? Melanie?"

Keo shoved me again, harder. I lost my balance and fell back into the door.

"Come on!" Keo, said calling me to him with his hands. "You the pantie."

I got up and dove at him, hitting him in the stomach with my shoulder. We fell back to his bed, then rolled off onto the floor, grunting, sputtering. He got me in a headlock and squeezed until I could feel my ears burn.

The door flew open and Aunty Pearl's voice boomed into the room.

"*Keo!*"

We lay on the floor still gripping each other, breathing hard.

"Sonny, you better go home now," Aunty Pearl said.

"Yeah, pantie," Keo added, spitting out the *pantie* part.

"You shut your mouth!" Aunty Pearl said. "You going stay this room till Daddy gets home."

I pulled myself free and backed away from Keo. Melanie stood behind Aunty Pearl, peeking around the door. I brushed by without looking at her and stomped out into the yard. My ears ached and the skin on my face felt as if I'd washed it with a burlap bag. It was the first big fight Keo and I had ever gotten into, and I hated him.

It was quiet down at my house with Dad gone. I made a peanut butter and banana sandwich and went out by the ocean to think about everything that had happened that day. The only thing I would have done differently was take Melanie's advice and have left Keo alone to cool off.

Later that evening the phone rang.

"Hi," Melanie said in a voice I recognized instantly. "What are you doing?"

"Not much. Just sitting around. Is Keo still all bent out of shape?"

"I don't know. I guess so."

I couldn't think of anything more to say. I hoped she'd come up with something, because I didn't want her to hang up.

"Aunty Pearl told him she wouldn't tell Uncle Harley about it if he'd apologize to me," she added.

"Did he?"

"Sort of. But I don't care. Aunty Pearl said he was too bullheaded for his own good."

"She's right about that."

"Let's do something tomorrow," Melanie said. "It's the only day Aunty Pearl hasn't planned something for me."

"What?"

"I don't know. How about swimming at the hotel?"

"You can only swim there if you're staying there," I told her.

She paused a moment, then said, "Wanna bet?"

The next day we met at Kona Inn, at the big saltwater swimming pool, just as we'd planned. But when she got there she didn't like it. "It's too crowded. Let's go somewhere more private."

I looked around, as if I were thinking of a place to go, but was really wondering what she had in mind by *more private*.

"Where can we go where there aren't any people around?" she asked.

I shrugged. "I don't know. Out by the airport?"

"Sounds good to me."

It was a long walk under a relentless sun, but worth every burning step. The thing about Melanie was that I couldn't ever tell what she was thinking. I got the feeling that when I wasn't looking at her, she was looking at me. It thrilled me to think that it might be true. But whenever I glanced at her, she'd turn away. Once, though, just before we got to the beach, I peeked over and she looked straight back at me, without hiding it. We both just stood there looking into each other's eyes. It made my breathing shallow.

Then she smiled, and turned away.

From then on I had to fight myself to keep from staring at her, because staring at her was everything in the world I wanted to do. Nothing else mattered. Anywhere.

"There's a big tidal pool just beyond those rocks," I said when we got out by the airport. "Not many people come this far to go swimming."

"Good," she said. "I hope no one's there now."

The pool was shallow and warm, almost too warm. And the beach around it was deserted. She waded in up to her knees, then reached down and lifted out a dripping handful of seawater. She studied the pool, the sand, and the rocks around it, and the blue, blue ocean beyond. I drifted off in my mind to some lost island in the deep South Pacific. We were shipwrecked—just the two of us.

I must have looked pretty dreamy, because Melanie splashed me. She glowed under a brilliant sun, wading back to shore. She ran back up on the sand and threw down her towel, then took off her shorts and blouse. Underneath, she wore a light green bikini that sent my mind reeling. "Come on," she said, running back into the water.

We lolled around in the tidal pool for a while, sitting on the bottom up to our necks, then swimming around slowly, like a couple of porpoises, bumping arms and talking about everything we could think of.

When my fingers started to shrivel up from being in the water so long, I got out and lay down on my stomach in the sand. The hot sun felt good on my back. Melanie got out, too, and lay next to me on her side, propped up on one elbow. She ran her fingertips over my back, lightly, in small swirls.

"Have you ever kissed a girl?" she asked.

I rolled over on my back. What kind of question was *that*?

She brushed the sand from my chest, like brushing dust off a table. "Come on, have you?"

"Sure," I said, which was a lie. I'd never even had a girlfriend. Keo sort of had one, but I didn't.

Melanie got up on her hands and knees and bent over me. I said nothing, stunned by her closeness.

Her hair fell around my face when she kissed me—damp, heavenly, engulfing hair. My mind swirled. My body seemed to float up off the earth, and spin, again and again. Her mouth was soft, squishy, silken. Tasting sweet. Was this really happening to *me*?

Then she rolled away and lay on her back with her eyes closed. We lay side by side for a long time, holding hands. We didn't say much, but my mind had started up again. I could have stayed there for the rest of my life.

Did Dad feel this way about my mother? If he did, it must have killed him when she died.

My thoughts drifted back to the lava tube, to the sound of Melanie's voice, her crying, her hand squeezing mine. Her father. Dad. We shared the same fear. No one else would ever know that.

I wanted the world to go away, to leave Melanie and me alone on the beach forever.

"Melanie . . ." I whispered.

She turned toward me and smiled.

I couldn't have stopped myself if I'd wanted to. I rolled over and kissed her, again and again, softly, gently, my tongue twirling around hers, my mind numb. I kissed her until my heart burst, until tears of unspeakable joy filled my eyes.

After Melanie had gone back to Honolulu she sent me a postcard. It was an old-time brown and white one with a photograph on the front of a young Hawaiian man and woman standing knee-deep in a mountain pond. A low waterfall emptied into it and a thick jungle of bamboo, ginger, and tall grass surrounded it. The woman was watching the man who was bent over with cupped hands, drinking from the pond.

When Dad handed me the card he gave me a funny look, but left it at that. I turned the postcard over to see who it was from, and when I read "Melanie" I took it out to the rocks by the water, alone except for the dogs who followed me. Before I read it, I sat looking at the ocean, at its crisp horizon, trying to slow my excitement. I wanted to read her card with no thoughts in my mind. I wanted a pure, white canvas to place a few strokes of color on.

I read the card perhaps fifteen or twenty times over, each time trying to find something new in it.

> *Dear Sonny,*
>
> *I still remember very clearly being alone with you in the cave, and how sad I felt, and how you tried to make me feel better. There is a small piece of plate on the desk next to me. Whenever I hold it in my hand I think of you. Right now I wish we were back on the beach at the tidal pool. You can write if you want. I'd like that very much.*
>
> > *Love,*
> > *Melanie*
>
> *P.S. How's pantie Keo? (ha, ha)*

Love, Melanie.

Down in the lower left-hand corner there was a caption for the photograph on the front that read, "Tiger Lily Pond, Island of Oahu, 1926." And below that Melanie had written, "That's you and me on the front."

I read the card every night before going to sleep, studying her words, dreaming over the picture of Tiger Lily Pond, smelling the fading fragrance of Melanie McNeil in the ink.

I wrote to her—long, mushy love letters that I couldn't control. Where it all came from, I didn't know. And Melanie wrote back, eight times. Eight letters that made up the extent of my entire world for more than three months.

Her father recovered, and Melanie seemed much happier. But her letters got breezy, thinner, lighter in their envelopes.

Then they stopped.

I wrote and wrote, but nothing happened. I went down to our post office box more times than in all my life before, and always came away feeling as if I'd swallowed a fishhook and someone was pulling up on it. I wanted to talk to Dad, but what could I say? My mother would have understood. Maybe.

8

The Boy in the Shadow

(1962)

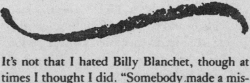

It's not that I hated Billy Blanchet, though at times I thought I did. "Somebody made a mistake," Uncle Raz had told Keo and me. "That boy belongs on another planet."

Billy was seventeen, three years older than me, and taller by at least three inches. And solid, with lots of muscle—sharp, molded chest, rippled stomach, and arms with protruding veins. He was of mixed blood, probably Hawaiian-French-Portuguese-Filipino, and maybe a little Japanese.

Many times I'd watched him fish with his bow and arrow off the seawall, crouching low, and studying the ocean, his eyes pinned on what he was after. When he crept in to strike, you didn't see a boy, you saw a cat. Quick, fluid, graceful. Physically, Billy Blanchet was everything I wanted to be.

He drifted around the harbor, appearing on the pier, then disappearing, and showing up somewhere else. At times he'd startle me when I'd suddenly notice him sitting still as stone against the wheel of a Jeep, or squatting in the broken shade of a palm tree, like a lizard hiding in the grain of a rock. He was always alone, and never without his bow.

The word around Kailua was that he was unpredictable, "unstable" Uncle Raz called him. Some people said it was just a matter of time. He'd be in prison before he was twenty-five, just like his brother.

What amazed me was that he could put an arrow through a fish ten yards off the seawall. He'd stand perfectly still for five or ten minutes watching fish move beneath the surface, becoming to them a tree or a rock. Then in the moment he seemed to be waiting for, he'd swing the bow up to his cheek and shoot with only the hint of an aim. He must have missed a time or two, but I only saw him do it once.

For several months now, ever since meeting Billy up at Keo's house, I'd started feeling almost sick inside at the way I'd try to disappear whenever I saw him. He hadn't threatened me, or even challenged me. I'd just left Keo's house *thinking* he had.

I'd gone there with Dad to put some fresh *ahi* in Uncle Harley's icehouse. The day was dry and hot. When Dad turned off the Jeep the place was so quiet I could hear old Alii grunting softly in his pigpen. The engine snapped and clicked as it cooled down. Dad went into the house to find Uncle Harley.

It was *too* quiet. No dogs. Bullet and Blossom were gone.

Aunty Pearl stood in the doorway. "Keo and Billy down Silva's lower pasture," she said. She smiled and started back inside.

"Wait. What Billy?"

"A boy from Kainaliu. Somebody Keo knows from school." Her smile faded. "He going stay with us for a while." Aunty Pearl went back into the house without telling me to come give her a hug. I didn't remember any Billy Keo knew at school.

I found them near an old, rusty steel water trough under a

towering mango tree in Silva's lower pasture. They were shooting at a piece of cardboard tacked to the tree. Someone had drawn three circles on it, target style. Keo was using Uncle Harley's twenty-two and Billy his bow. Silva's cows were clumped together downhill, staring at them from the corner of the pasture.

"Keo," I called, squeezing through the barbed-wire fence. Bullet and Blossom started a wave of barking, and ran over with their tails wagging.

The barking startled Billy. He spun around quickly and glared over at me from the shadow of the mango tree. *That* Billy.

"Aay, Sonny," Keo called. "Come shoot." He turned back toward the tree and fired off a round, but Billy kept his eyes on me. He wore a white T-shirt and camouflage army fatigues. Barefoot, like Keo and me.

"This is Billy," Keo said after I'd crossed the pasture. "He ran away from home."

Billy studied me.

He had a large bruise on his cheek and a cut on his arm, just above the elbow. It was scabby, and had stitches in it. A conspicuous scar slashed through his left eyebrow, a thin river of flesh where hair should have been.

I'd seen him at school, mostly lurking around by himself. He didn't have any friends that I knew of. He was too *weird*. But I guess Keo, being only a tenth grader, felt pretty big about having an eleventh grade friend.

I reached out to shake as Dad had told me to do whenever I met someone. Billy didn't move. I was just about to drop my hand when he grabbed it. His grip was incredible, like pliers.

"Sheese!" I said, trying to pull my hand away. But he wouldn't let go.

"Billy!" Keo said.

Billy let up on the pressure, then let go, and smiled. "You shake like a lady," he said.

I rubbed my hand and glanced over at Keo, then back at Billy. There was no way to answer an insult like that without starting a fight. Already I hated him.

"Are you a lady or a man?" Billy asked. His voice sounded strangely soft, not edgy or irritating, like you'd think it would be. His words cut ice-pick deep, but his tone was almost soothing. When neither Keo nor I answered, he said, "I know, you're a lady-man," then snickered at his own clever words.

Keo held his rifle sideways across his chest, barrel pointing up into the leaves. It was so quiet at that altitude you could hear mosquitoes. Keo and I waited, neither of us knowing what to do.

Billy shifted. "Lady-man, watch."

He backed away from the target, fifty or sixty feet. Keo and I moved to the side as Billy set an arrow into the bow and stood holding it in place with one hand, point to the ground.

For at least thirty seconds he concentrated on the target, never even blinking his eyes. He raised the bow and shot. I barely saw him pull back the bowstring. The arrow thwacked into the tree and vibrated. As much as I didn't like Billy, I was speechless with awe when I saw that he'd hit the target dead center.

Keo and I must have looked paralyzed. Billy laughed, not in a chilling way, but a laugh that sounded like he wasn't that bad.

Billy held the bow out to me. "You want to try?"

"No, but I'll shoot the twenty-two."

Keo handed me the rifle and I walked back to where Billy had shot from. I tried to imitate what Billy had done, raising the rifle quickly, and shooting without aiming.

I missed the target *and* the tree.

The horn on Dad's Jeep honked, and the dogs ran toward the house. "I have to go," I said. "See you, Keo." I glanced at Billy and nodded. He flicked his eyebrows and said, "Better put some muscle into that hand."

Billy stayed with Aunty Pearl and Uncle Harley for a week before his father came looking for him. Mr. Blanchet, Aunty Pearl had learned from Billy's mother, had a problem with drinking, a big problem, getting drunk and beating up on Billy, like he'd done to Billy's older brother. Billy's mother cried when she'd spoken to Aunty Pearl, painfully thankful that her son had somewhere to go.

But Mr. Blanchet found out where Billy was and came to get him in the middle of the night.

When Billy heard the pounding on the door he snapped out of bed and ran from one side of Keo's room to the other, back and forth, looking for a place to hide. Uncle Harley was out night fishing with Uncle Raz, and Aunty Pearl had to get up and quiet the noise. Keo said he thought the door would crash down into the house. It scared him so much his heart nearly pounded out of his chest.

Aunty Pearl told Billy's father to settle down, but he was too far gone to reason with. He pushed by her and stumbled into every room in the house looking for Billy. Keo said the whites of his eyes were yellow, and he smelled like two weeks on a tuna boat without a bath.

Billy rolled under his bed and curled up against the wall just before his father busted into Keo's room and started tearing the place apart. He pulled the bed out and flipped it over. The first thing he did was slug Billy in the face and tell him to get back home where he had things to do. Keo said the sound of Mr. Blanchet's fist hitting Billy's cheek made him sick to his stomach. Aunty Pearl tried to stop him but could only slow him down by pushing and moving her body between them. Billy ran out behind her.

Aunty Pearl cried for hours that night, Keo said. And it took days to get rid of the scent of Billy's father.

Less than a month later Billy ran away again, this time staying somewhere else. His mother called Aunty Pearl, but none of us knew where he was, except that Uncle Raz had seen him around the pier a couple of times, fishing with his bow. We figured he was living off what he caught.

Keo pointed Billy's father out to me one day when he saw him coming out of the bar at Ocean View Inn. Uncle Harley told us to steer clear of him. He was sour enough when he was sober, and he might even accuse us of hiding Billy.

One afternoon, about three weeks after we'd heard that Billy had run away again, I was down at the pier waiting for Dad to come in from fishing. The white sky and muggy air made the insides of my arms sticky, a hot, thick day, the kind where you never get to feeling comfortable. I went over to the cove on the far side of the pier and sank down into the ocean to cool off. When I came up out of the water I saw a man lying on his side, curled under a palm tree just above the beach.

There were always one or two strangers hanging around town, "bums" Uncle Raz called them, wandering men, mostly. Keo and I usually left them alone, though sometimes we'd talk to them because they almost always had wild stories to tell of places they'd seen and trouble they'd had. But this man didn't seem like one of them. He wasn't as grimy as they were.

I crept up to the palm tree, keeping my distance, studying the still body, wondering if the man was more dead than alive. His chest rose and fell slowly behind his knees, which were pulled up close to him, his hands between them.

He mumbled something, then opened his eyes to a strained squint. He tried to get up. An ugly splotch of dried blood swelled above his left eye. He fell back down and groaned.

"Mister," I said, from a few feet away. "Are you all right?"

The man mumbled again and rolled his eyes up at me. He reached out a hand, but I backed away when I saw that he was Billy's father.

"Do you need help?" I asked. "Sh-should I get some help?"

"Boy . . ." he said, then he fell back.

I moved closer, keeping just out of reach, and could see that he'd passed out. He smelled like beer, worse than beer, whiskey or something, and sweat. He must have gotten into a fight.

"Mister," I said.

When he didn't move, I went around behind him and lifted him to a sitting position, leaning him against the tree, then ran over to Dad's Jeep and got an old rag. I soaked it in fresh water from a spigot on the pier.

He woke up while I was dabbing at the blood on his forehead. I jumped away but crept back up to him when I saw that he didn't even have the energy to hold his own head up.

"You got a bad bump, Mr. Blanchet," I said.

Suddenly, someone knelt down next to me, and pushed me away.

Billy.

He must have been watching his father, keeping his distance.

He took the wet rag from my hand when I offered it to him and wiped his father's face, as if giving him a sponge bath, working silently, scowling. He was careful when he came close to the cut, patting it gently, trying to clean out the dirt. A crude tattoo that I hadn't noticed before scarred the fleshy part of Billy's hand, between his thumb and first finger, a dark cross with a dot in each quarter.

Mr. Blanchet opened his eyes. When he saw Billy, he half smiled, and said, ". . . shit."

Billy ignored him and straightened his father's clothes, making him look as neat as he could. Then he sat back on his heels and stared at him. Wavelets plopped up on the sand in the cove, rolling pebbles around in a rush of small, familiar clicking sounds.

Mr. Blanchet passed out again, his chin resting on his chest. Billy and I both watched every unsteady breath Mr. Blanchet took as if it would be his last.

The fishing boats were coming in—Dad would be back soon. When I got up to leave, Billy glanced up at me, his eyes looking half swollen, as if he'd been awake for days. He said nothing, then turned back to his father.

Keo had started going out with Bobby Otani's little sister, Cheryl, an eighth grader. She was as bossy as Tutu Max and I couldn't see what he liked about her, except that she was pretty good-looking. I hardly ever saw Keo anymore. The two of them just seemed to get lost in the trees and rocks and beaches, like ghosts.

But Billy Blanchet didn't disappear so easily.

I was fishing alone one day, near the palace, now a museum made out of the old Hawaiian royal residence. It sat in a grove of tall coconut trees in the middle of the village, a white, two-story building facing the ocean.

I'd gotten there early, hoping the fish would be feeding, casting my spinner off the rock wall that edged a small mullet pond just south of the palace. The pond was part of the museum, and the lazy mullet in its clear water were protected by law.

The narrow wall I stood on fell about five feet to the ocean on one side, and even farther into the mullet pond on the other. I peeked back into the pond every now and then, tempted to go after a couple of forbidden fish, fat gray creatures hanging over shadows that followed them around on the silty bottom.

Then I saw Billy.

He was crouching on the seawall that curved around the bay on the other side of the palace grounds. He was as easy to spot as a shark in shallow water. A small wave of dread rolled through my stomach.

Between casts I glanced back toward the seawall. I still stung from the way he'd shamed me in front of Keo, calling me lady-man. Although he hadn't called me anything the time I ran into his father, I still hated him for it.

When I looked up again, Billy was gone. I scanned the entire seawall until it ended, then studied the small colors and shapes on the pier to see if he was there. He never wore anything but a white T-shirt and camouflage fatigues. And, of course, there was the bow.

I wasn't paying attention to the spinner when it snagged in the reef. "Damn!" I said, whipping the rod back and forth, the line whistling in the air. I couldn't free the hook. I paced back and forth pulling and snapping the rod against the snag, and was so skittish about Billy being in town that I flinched when I suddenly saw him at the end of the mullet pond, watching me.

Filipino-style, he squatted low to the ground, feet flat, sitting with his arms on his knees, stretched out in front of him. He held the bow in his left hand.

"Lady-man," he said, just loud enough for me to hear. He flicked his eyebrows up and down quickly, without moving another muscle in his body. "You fish like you shoot," he said.

I pretended to ignore him and continued trying to unsnag the line.

Billy stood and came up to me, walking slowly along the top of the wall. There was no way he could pass. It was less than two feet wide. He came so close I could smell him, not a bad smell, but distinctive, tangy, like the smell of rust. Heat radiated off his body, like it comes off the side of a building in the afternoon.

Billy's eyes could drill into you. You could see every ounce of his power in them. The whites were clear and bright as sunlight. But the part that got you was the dark part—the deep brown-black—the iris. It almost filled the eye. They came at you like a couple of his arrows. "Why you waste time doing that?" he said.

I stopped jerking on the line and held it taut, rod bowed out over the ocean. Billy pulled a pocket knife from his fatigues and opened it, hanging his bow over his left shoulder. The line was stiff and snapped easily when he touched it with the razor-sharp blade.

I said nothing.

He took the bow off his shoulder and pulled an arrow from the small rawhide quiver attached to his belt. "I show you how."

I backed away a couple of steps and faced him. He was left-handed and had a left-handed bow. On the right side of his belt was a length of nylon fishing line, heavy gauge, looped several times and hanging to his knee. He clipped the line to a small eye on the arrow, and set the arrow into the bow, resting it on his right thumb. Billy thought for a few seconds, then spun around and shot.

The arrow whacked a mullet in the palace pond, entering its head just behind the eyes. The mullet simply stopped all signs of life and sank.

"Look," he said softly, in an almost fatherly way. "Easy."

Billy pulled the fish up by the line attached to the arrow. The mullet was about a foot and a half long. He held it up close to my face.

"Look at the eyes," he said. "He never knew I was there." Billy pushed the dead fish off the arrow and let it fall back into the pond. The school of mullet scattered as it sank and floated back up, on its belly.

Billy looked me over. "Come, lady-man, I like show you something." He pointed beyond me with his bow.

I'd learned that the best way to avoid trouble was to keep

from making too much eye contact, and to relax, as if nothing out of the ordinary was going on. To act perfectly calm in a tight situation seemed to let some of the air out of a threat.

I shrugged and walked along the wall in the direction he'd pointed, following the rocky shoreline through the manicured grounds of Kona Inn into a dense grove of coconut trees on the other side.

He took me to a clearing deep in the grove.

"This is good," he said.

I heard cars driving by on the road nearby but saw nothing through the trees and brush, not even the hotel.

"Yes, this is a good place, lady-man."

Not making eye contact was easy. But trying to act calm when you're scared so bad your tongue goes dry is a tough thing to do.

I leaned my fishing rod against one of the trees. Billy poked with his foot at the coconuts lying in the sand under fallen palm fronds.

"You want to shoot the bow?" Billy asked. A command, not a question. I glanced around the grove for a way to run if I had to, trying not to look as scared as I felt.

"Sure," I said, acting easy, as if I were talking to Keo. Billy smiled. I think he didn't expect me to go for it.

"Good, lady-man. I'll make a target."

He handed me the bow. It was shiny, lacquered black with natural wood-grained edges, and the grip was carved to curl around a right hand. It was a lot lighter than it looked. I wondered if I was the only other person in the world to have touched it. The bow string was tight, like the feel of a one-hundred-twenty-pound test line with a five-hundred-pound marlin on it. It was beautiful, but it was a left-handed bow. The grip was off. I became aware of the low rumbling sound of waves along the rocky shoreline behind me. I should have gone spear fishing.

"Nice bow," I said. "But I can't shoot it. I'm right-handed."

"How's this?" He held up a large coconut, a dried out brown one.

"I'm right-handed," I repeated, a little louder. "Can't shoot a left-handed bow."

He wasn't listening, and wasn't going to. I would shoot the bow. Any feelings I had of him being like any other person disappeared.

"Shoot this." He held the coconut above his head, then pulled an arrow from his quiver and tossed it to me.

I gripped the backward bow as well as I could in my left hand, then set the feathered end of the arrow into the bow-string. I'd do what I could. I'd shot a bow before, but it had been a while.

Then I looked up to where he'd placed the target.

"What are you doing?"

"Shoot the coconut, lady-man."

Up against the trunk of a coconut tree, Billy stood with his arms crossed in front of him . . . with the brown coconut sitting on his head.

I gawked at him with the arrow at rest in the bow.

"Shoot!"

"I . . . No . . ."

I'd hit him—I'd hit him if I shoot this. Even with a right-handed bow I'd probably miss the coconut. Somebody come by, somebody please come by and break up this insane game. Somebody . . .

"Shoot or I'll bust your ass! Shoot!"

He was crazy, everyone knew it. I wanted to throw the bow into the ocean and run like hell.

"*Shoot!*"

I lifted the bow and shot, deliberately aiming off to the right of the tree. Billy slammed the coconut to the ground and came at me. He stared straight into my eyes, inches away, breathing hard, his breath sour, and his face tight. "One more chance, punk—one."

Without letting up on his stare, he gave me another arrow, then walked back to the tree. He held his arms out to the side of his body as he moved. Billy put the coconut back on his head and waited.

"Okay," he said. "Shoot."

Again, I slipped the arrow into the bow and pulled back. The shaft felt smooth and precise as it slid slowly along my thumb.

I closed one eye, aimed at the coconut, and shot.

The arrow hit in an instant, as fast as Keo's twenty-two. It glanced off the lower left corner of the coconut and sank into Billy's thick hair, stopping with a thud in the coconut tree. I held my breath. If I hadn't hit him, I'd come damn close.

Billy smiled. Slowly. He reached up and pushed the coconut off his head, and holding very still worked the arrow from the tree while keeping his eyes on me.

"Good," he said. "Now it's my turn."

I lowered the bow.

It looked as if I'd barely missed him, but I didn't feel any relief. He came toward me, stopping for a moment to pick up a much smaller coconut, about the size of a mango. He handed it to me and took back the bow.

I held the coconut at my waist and looked down at it, brushing an ant off the husk.

"On your head, lady-man. By the tree."

My fear seemed numbed, oddly hypnotized. I walked to the tree, put the small coconut on my head, and waited.

Billy smiled and raised the bow leisurely, totally unlike the way he went after the mullet. He drew the arrow back and held it. I watched the tip move down from the target on my head, to a point on my face, to my neck, my chest. I stood absolutely still. It wasn't a matter of hitting the coconut. It could have been the size of a fish eye and he'd have hit it. Billy Blanchet wanted my fear.

He stepped back, still holding the arrow in the bow, and still aiming at the center of my chest. Behind me cars moaned by, muffled by the trees. Billy looked at me through one open eye, down the shaft of the arrow.

His hands seemed to be shaking, the bow moving in small jerks from side to side. Then he brought the tip of the arrow back up to my head and shot.

I closed my eyes at the very moment I heard the heavy *thwack*, then dropped to my knees, raising my hands to my head. The coconut was impaled on the tree, hit dead center, milk seeping out around the edge of the arrow's shaft.

Billy strode up without so much as a glance at me, taking long strides. He pulled the arrow from the tree and stripped away the coconut, his skin shiny with a sheen of sweat.

Afraid to even breathe, I waited on my knees as he walked away.

For a moment the world narrowed down to the area around the back of his head. Nothing seemed to move but the weaving of his white T-shirt vanishing into the trees. I couldn't take my eyes off the bobbing red blotch stained into the shoulder of his shirt just below a thin trail of blood that ran out of his hair down the back of his neck.

I saw him several times again, around the pier, and on the seawall shooting fish. And though a slight twinge went off in my stomach every time I saw him, I stopped crossing the street to avoid him. He seemed to have forgotten me and Keo, something we greeted with great thankfulness.

But Billy showed up at my house one Sunday, near sunset. I

was out casting off the rocks for *moi*. Dad was at the house working on his outboard, which he'd set into a fifty-gallon drum of water. The engine hummed and smoke rose out of the drum like a huge vat of boiling crabs.

I felt Billy before I saw him. I don't know how long he'd been there, about ten yards away. He was staring into the sea with an arrow at rest in the bow. How he'd gotten there without Dad's dogs picking up on it completely baffled me.

Billy raised his bow, aiming into the water. He stood perfectly still for long minutes, concentrating. Then slowly he pulled back on the bowstring, light and easy, as if it had the resistance of a dove's feather. The arrow pierced the water with a small glooping sound, fishing line racing in behind it.

We both watched the point where the arrow had entered the water, the fishing line seeming to race into a hundred quivering fathoms of ocean. He seemed kind of dreamy, different from the Billy Blanchet in the coconut grove.

When the line went limp, he pulled it back, taking his time. He recovered the arrow and ran it between his thumb and finger to dry it. No fish.

Only after he'd detached the line and placed the arrow back into the quiver did he look over at me. He smiled and flicked his eyebrows, and said, "Missed."

He hopped over the rocks, light and as surefooted as the dogs. He stopped a few feet away, then looked out over the water. "I'm getting out of this place," he said after a long silence.

Back at the house Dad had shut down the outboard. I glanced back to see if he was still outside. Billy looked back at Dad, too, waiting for me to say something.

"Where are you going?"

"Any place but here." He set one tip of his bow on his foot so it wouldn't get scratched by the rocks, then bent the back and disengaged the bowstring. He ran his hand along the black lacquered bow.

"Sonny," he said, the sound of my name as startling as suddenly noticing him sitting frozen in a shadow. "Take care of this for me."

Billy removed the quiver from his waist and gave that to me, too. Without the bow, he seemed somehow smaller.

"I got a ride on a boat, but they said I can't take the bow. I guess they don't trust me or something." He paused, thinking, I suppose, about what he'd just said. Then he reached out to shake.

The last time he'd nearly crushed my hand. I hesitated, but he kept his hand out until I took it. We shook. His grip was solid, but he didn't force it.

Billy let go and started to walk away, then stopped. His eyes drilled me again, like at the mullet pond. But this time there was no anger in them.

I stared back and he blinked, shifted his eyes, then quickly fixed them on me again.

"Punk. A lady-man would not have let me shoot at him," he said, and walked away.

The next day Billy shipped out on a commercial tuna boat. His father was mad as hell when he found out. He stayed in Kailua for more than a week stumbling around the pier and babbling about his no-good son.

A few months later I unrolled the beautifully crafted black bow from the old canvas tarp that I kept it in. I tested its resiliency, resting an arrow against my thumb and pulling back. I took it into the trees and shot arrows into a cardboard box, wondering where Billy was, and how he was doing.

"He's not a bad boy," Aunty Pearl said after he'd gone. "There are just so many things that boy doesn't know. He was asking for help and making a mess of it, that's all. In his heart he wanted to reach out." And though Keo and I, and even Uncle Raz, had our doubts, she kept to that view.

Still, Billy had made me shoot an arrow at him knowing that I couldn't handle a bow for beans. And I'd let him shoot at me. There was a lot more to it than reaching out. It was something deeper, and something warlike. And scary, even for Billy. Maybe that's why he ran away.

Blue Skin of the Sea

(1963)

One morning Keo and I took Dad's skiff two miles offshore and closed the engine down. We both wanted to know what it was like to swim in silence over a hundred fathoms of water, with nothing but our bodies and one small boat to count on.

I swam around the skiff, never more than a few yards away. The ocean was deep, deep blue, and flat. But it wasn't the peaceful place I thought it would be. It snapped and clicked, eerie staticlike sounds rising from a billion living things below.

The ocean itself, its endlessness and its strength, was warm and comforting, but thoughts of what lurked beneath my feet were like flies that wouldn't be batted away. After years on the water there was still something that made me fear and doubt the ocean as if its one goal was to pull me down and swallow me. And there were those thoughts, or dream-memories—*Calm down, now . . . it was nothing . . .*

I headed back to the skiff and pulled myself aboard.

Keo swam out toward the horizon until he was nothing but a black speck. He turned and waved for me to follow him. I waved back and pointed into the boat, as if there were something important there I had to do.

Keo kept on waving. Nothing about swimming out there bothered him in the least. But I felt as if it would suck me down into its lightless depths, into the hungry mouths of gigantic sharks. I lay in the cradle of the skiff with my hands behind my head and feet up on the stern seat.

"What's the matter," Keo said, pulling himself over the side of the skiff. "It's wild out there, spooky. You can see only the top half of the island. Why didn't you come out?"

"I got a cramp," I said, rubbing my leg. "I had to get back in the boat and work it out."

"Shee," Keo said. "You lie like a fish in a frying pan."

"Okay, I just didn't like the feel of it. Could be sharks out here." I thought about telling him about my dreams, but didn't. It would only give him more reason to laugh at me.

I moved to the stern and pumped some gas into the outboard, then pulled the cord and got it going. White smoke blossomed out of the bubbling water, smelling sweet and sickening at the same time.

"Could be," he said, yelling over the sudden noise of the engine. "And could be sharks in by shore, too."

He turned his back to me, not seeming disgusted, but as if he were feeling sorry for me. Somehow things were changing between us. Maybe it was because of Cheryl Otani and the way Keo was so absorbed by her. She didn't let him get away with very much. But Keo never complained. In fact, he seemed to like how she kept her eye on him. She would have driven me crazy.

But maybe it wasn't because of her at all.

*　　*　　*

A week later Keo got his driver's license and came down to my house to take me for a ride to the pier in Uncle Harley's Jeep. I had my permit and was itching to get behind the wheel myself, but he wouldn't stop and switch places no matter how much I begged. I glared off into the trees. He'd better let me drive on the way back.

When we got down past Emma's Store people were crowded all along the seawall, from the palace to the pier, looking down into the water. Keo drove along the road behind them and parked by the banyan tree in front of Taneguchi's. We ran over and squeezed into the crowd.

"Look at *that*!" Keo whispered.

An enormous tiger shark loomed just inches below the surface, circling around the bay, first passing below us, then meandering over to the pier on the right, then out toward the nearest mooring, and back in again. It moved slowly, tail wafting lazily from side to side like a palm in a morning breeze.

I'd never seen a shark in the bay before, and had never in my life seen one as big as this—more than half the length of Dad's sampan. The sun spread flickering silver dollars of light over its gray skin as it glided by a second time.

I whispered to Keo, "I wonder what brought him in here."

"Someone must have dumped a lot of fish guts." Keo rubbed the side of his arm, as if he were cold, and kept his eye on the shark.

"Maybe it's sick."

The shark swam by the pier one last time, its dorsal silently cutting the water. It angled out toward the moorings and disappeared under the thin blue skin of the sea.

"Come on," Keo said, losing interest. "Let's take the Jeep out to the airport, then up to the dump."

"Give me the key," I said, reaching out. "It's my turn to drive."

Keo scowled. "I said later. You want to come along or what."

He turned and jogged over to the Jeep without looking back to see if I was following him, but waited after starting it. I took my time getting there.

About noon we drove back down to Kailua. We'd gone to the airport, then to the dump, then up Palani Road to where it meets Mamalahoa. Keo drove the whole time.

We ran into Uncle Harley on the pier. He'd been meeting with some of the charter boat skippers and hotel managers. Something had to be done about the shark, he said. People were afraid to go in the water. "If it hangs around too long we're going to have some empty hotel rooms, and what if it came back and someone was swimming, or out spear fishing? We need help. I'm going down to Honaunau to get Deeps . . . want to come along?"

Of course, we did. The name "Deeps" wasn't one people used freely around town, though I'd heard every story ever told about "shark-killer" Deeps. And like sharks, people feared him based on reputation, accurate or not. Dad said he was either the bravest or stupidest man alive.

"Someone has to kill the thing," Uncle Harley said as we drove through the village. "You just can't take a chance on it coming back and hurting someone." He paused, thinking. "What I can't figure out is what attracted it." Uncle Harley puffed up his cheeks and blew out the air, tapping the steering wheel with his thumb.

Keo sat in the middle of the truck cab between me and Uncle Harley. The whole way up the hill and south through the Kona highlands he blabbed on about how to catch the shark and kill it. You'd have thought *he* was the one who was going to hire Deeps.

After about an hour Uncle Harley turned seaward and

dropped down to the coast. "Keep your eyes out for an old shack with shark jaws all over it."

The lush highland jungle dried into brittle trees and brown grasses, and the coolness in the air evaporated quickly once we reached sea level.

Keo saw it first.

What sounded like twenty dogs exploded in a frenzy of barking as we pulled into the rock and weed yard. I rolled up the window on my side of the cab even though my T-shirt was glued to my back. Those kind of hunting dogs don't care *who* you are, dogs bred half crazy to their brothers and sisters and trained to be mean—usually short-haired, mostly pit bull mixtures, gray with black spots, breedless. No finer hunting dogs existed, Dad would say. But they would eat your heart right out of your chest if they found the smell of blood and fear on you.

Uncle Harley turned off the ignition. The dogs, actually only six of them, leaped at the windows, raising lips and showing teeth and yapping as if they hadn't seen anyone around the place for years.

"Deeps!" Uncle Harley called. He didn't roll up his window, but he pulled his arm in.

The door to the shack was open, but it was too dark inside to see anything. On the outside no less than thirty shark jaws hung on nails, some small, some huge, all pried open, with full sets of teeth slicing out at you.

Uncle Harley called again, louder, the dogs worked into a frenzy by now. "*Deeps*, you home?"

A dog yelped, then another, both hit by small stones. The barking broke up, then stopped and turned into agitated whining. From somewhere behind the truck, Deeps called off his dogs, keeping back as if he thought someone might leap out of the cab. I watched him in the mirror on Uncle Harley's door.

He studied us for a moment, then came up to Uncle Harley's side of the truck and squinted into the cab at Keo and me.

I'd expected someone bigger, maybe a pockmarked face, or thick beard. But he was short and wiry. And bald as a porpoise, wearing only a baggy pair of dirty khaki pants. The lines shooting out from his eyes were sharp, cut deep into the skin from a lifetime in the sun. Long, wispy strands of hair drooped down from his chin like limp fishing line.

"We need you in Kailua," Uncle Harley said quietly, with respect. "A tiger shark, maybe twelve, thirteen feet, hanging around the harbor. We'll give you twenty-five cents a pound for it. Could weigh over a thousand."

The dogs paced back and forth on either side of the truck. Beads of sweat streamed down from my hair. I opened my window a couple of inches.

Deeps's face remained blank.

Then Uncle Harley added, "I can guarantee fifty bucks, catch 'um or not."

Deeps turned and went into his shack, two dogs following him. The others decided to stay and keep an eye on us.

"What's he doing?" Keo whispered.

"Hang on," Uncle Harley said. "He'll come with us. He's *lolo* as his dogs, but he'll come. All I had to say was *shark*."

Deeps came back out into the sunshine carrying a five-gallon plastic bucket full of lines and hooks, and a long aluminum pole. He put them in the bed of the truck, then went back into the shack. The heat in the cab was almost unbearable, even with the windows open, but no one wanted to get out.

Deeps came back with a handful of meat scraps and threw them on the ground. The dogs growled and snapped at each other, fighting over them. Then Deeps climbed over the tailgate into the truck. Keo and I turned and watched him settle down with his back to the cab.

Uncle Harley started the truck and headed up the mountain into the cool highlands. Deeps hadn't even closed the door to his shack.

It was past five o'clock when we got back down to the pier. The charter boats were in and twenty or thirty tourists were standing around taking pictures of a marlin hanging from the fish hoist. Dad and Uncle Raz sat facing the crowd on a low, wood rail on the cove side of the pier. They'd already cleaned their boats and moored them for the night.

"You hear about the tiger that came into the bay this morning?" Uncle Harley asked, sitting down on the rail next to Dad.

"Yep," Dad said. "Still around?"

Dad lifted his chin to Deeps, his way of saying hello. Uncle Raz did the same. Deeps ducked his head slightly.

"I need a boat and some fish," Deeps said, slapping the flat side of a steel hook against the palm of his hand. He turned around to spit after he spoke.

His high, thin voice surprised me.

Uncle Raz pushed himself up and went over to his truck. He pulled out a fair-sized tuna by the tail, about forty pounds. "This enough?"

Deeps nodded.

"You can use my skiff," Dad said.

Deeps glanced down at Dad's eight-foot skiff floating silently just off the wooden deck below the main pier. The outboard was still on the transom.

"Sonny," Dad said. "Go pull the skiff in."

I dropped down to the lower level and brought it alongside the landing. Deeps followed and climbed aboard. Uncle Raz handed him the tuna and the pole and bucket of hooks and cable that Deeps had brought.

I coiled up the stern line and was about to throw it out to Deeps when he turned to Uncle Harley.

"I need the boy," he said.

Uncle Harley's eyes shifted to me, then to Dad.

"I want to go, too." Keo dropped down onto the wooden deck.

"No," Deeps said. "I just need someone to run the boat."

Keo came up and stood next to me. "I can run it," Keo said, "and . . ."

Deeps waved his hand. "This boy better, smaller. I need the room."

Keo glared at me. I shrugged my shoulders.

Dad nodded, a look that told me to go ahead.

Keo began pacing.

Deeps put the bucket in the bow and tucked the pole under the seats. "Let's go," he said, "unless you afraid, and then I take the other boy."

"Let *me* go," Keo said. "I can run the boat, and I'm not afraid of sharks like he is."

Deeps looked up at me from the skiff.

"Ready when you are," I said.

Keo spun around and stalked off. I pushed the boat away from the pier and jumped in.

The outboard caught and I headed out beyond the end of the pier and into the open harbor where scattered fishing boats slept at their moorings.

"Go 'round one time," Deeps said, pointing into the bay where the shark had been. There was maybe an hour of sunlight left. He studied the surface of the water as we circled in near the seawall. A small group of people watched from the pier. Keo stood on a chock with a pair of binoculars.

"It's probably miles from here by now," I said.

Deeps nudged the tuna with his bare foot and smiled. "Fish guts bring 'um back."

A couple of minutes later Deeps said, "Did you see it?"

"Yes."

"Tell me about it."

"It was big, about twelve feet long. It circled around the bay twice, slowly, like it was just checking the place out. Then it went under, and that's it."

Deeps pointed to the farthest buoy. "Go to that white float," he said, then started digging through his bucket. I brought up the throttle and headed out.

The long aluminum pole stuck out from under the seat, its point resting on the bow. I studied it, trying to figure out what it was.

"For kill shark," Deeps said, without looking up. He reached over and ran his hand along the barrel. "Twelve-gauge powerhead, better than a cannon. Poke 'um on the back. The shell goes off and breaks the spine. Makes about twelve inches of mashed potatoes. But if you miss, the shark gets mad as hell."

When we got to the buoy, I slowed and grabbed it, then killed the engine. Deeps waited for the sun to go down and the sky to darken. I sat facing him, thinking about what Keo had said. *Afraid.*

Calm down, now . . . you're not a baby anymore.

On the pier, I could barely make Keo out, now sitting on the hood of Uncle Harley's Jeep with the binoculars, though I doubted he could see anything. Dad, Uncle Raz, and Uncle Harley were probably standing around talking in the dark somewhere.

Deeps finally spoke. "Give me the fish."

I stood and lifted the tuna over the center seat. Deeps, a dark gray shadow in the reflected light from shore, pointed to the floorboards by his feet. "Put 'um there." Then after a pause, he said, "What's your name, boy?"

"Sonny Mendoza."

"Raymond's boy."

I nodded.

"You ever see a shark eat a man?"

"No."

"Ugly thing. I work long time on a Japanee sampan. Off Kauai, one day, me and a Hawaiian guy was under the boat fixing the prop and three sharks came by. Not big like this one, but big enough. The boat was *loaded*, plenty fish inside the hold—the sharks could smell 'um."

He chopped half the tuna into fine chum as he spoke, then dumped everything out of his bucket onto the floorboards and put the guts and chum into it.

"The two of us came out from under the boat," Deeps went on. "We yelling to the guys on top—*Pull us up! Pull us up!* First they pull me, then they pull the Hawaiian guy, but one shark come grab the leg. I never hear one man scream like that before."

"What happened to him?"

"The sharks ate 'um."

Deeps put a huge chunk of raw meat on a hook attached to about three feet of chain, which was then connected to fifteen or twenty feet of steel cable, and threw it all over the side of the skiff. Then he churned the chum into a mushy mixture in the bucket and threw it out into the water. He washed his hands and the bucket in the ocean and told me to head back to the pier. We left the bait line attached to the buoy.

Fiery light from torches on the grounds of the King Kam Hotel reflected over the water in long, shimmering spears as we pulled up to the small boat landing. A cigarette glowed in the group of shadowy men milling around waiting for us.

Keo squatted on his heels on the lower dock. Uncle Harley gave Deeps a blanket and a beer. I guess Deeps would sleep on the beach.

Deeps walked by me and said, "We check 'um in the morning, boy. About seven." Then he took his blanket over to the far side of the sandy cove into a small grove of palm trees.

"What was going on out there?" Uncle Raz asked.

"Sitting around, waiting for dark to set the bait."

Keo wandered over, and within a couple of minutes, he was doing all the talking. "We could have done that without Deeps," he said. "It's the same as when we caught the shark out by the lighthouse."

"This one is three times bigger," I said.

"Sheese," Keo said, wanting me to think he had all the answers.

"Setting the bait is the easy part," Uncle Raz said, breaking into Keo's complaining. "Tomorrow you're gonna see why he's here. When you're messing with a big shark you don't want any mistakes."

That night I gasped myself awake, popping up on one elbow in a sweat. I dreamed that I was in the skiff, buzzing out into the harbor with a dog that wouldn't stop yapping at the water. Then the engine went dead, as if it had run out of gas. The dog got even more crazy and barked louder and louder. I peered into the water to see what he was so excited about. Instantly, a shark was charging up at me, rolling over, its eyelids closing and its cavernous mouth opening. *Don't ever do that again, boy . . . calm down, now . . . you're not a baby anymore.* The shark slammed the skiff, and sent the dog and me flying. I woke up when I hit the water. *It's okay . . . it was nothing . . . it was nothing.*

I couldn't get back to sleep for an hour.

Keo banged on my door at six o'clock. We got to the pier at six-thirty, Keo trying to look as smooth as Uncle Harley behind the wheel of the Jeep. He still hadn't let me drive.

We parked on the pier, the sun an hour from breaking over

the top of the mountain. Dad had gone down to the harbor long before.

I felt a little dizzy and the palms of my hands sweated.

Deeps stood on the pier with the blanket folded under his arm, gazing out toward the buoy. Dad sat with Uncle Harley in his truck, drinking coffee. I went down to the skiff and Keo went over to talk to them.

Deeps and I hummed past the end of the pier into the harbor, the water calm, almost glassy. Through the thin hull of the skiff the ocean felt like a sheet running under my feet. A sheet to wrap a dead body in—the parts the shark might leave behind.

I shut the engine down when we got to the buoy. Deeps worked up the cable.

The bait was gone.

Deeps looked off toward the horizon, running his finger over the edge of the steel hook. He coiled his cable and chain neatly into the bucket. "Let's go back," he said, quietly.

He spent the rest of the day squatting on the seawall watching the water.

That evening Deeps set his line again, but this time with a hunk of beef and two eight-inch steel hooks and four five-gallon buckets of cow guts from a slaughterhouse up the hill.

When we went out to the buoy the next morning the cable held. Deeps smiled and winked at me.

I squinted into the water, but couldn't see anything. I shuddered deep inside, the dream with the dog still haunting me.

Deeps began pulling the cable in.

"We got him," he whispered, the lines on his forehead furled into a tight scowl. The muscles in his neck stood out like strands of wire, and the cable around his fists made the skin go white. "This one's big as a cane truck."

A dark mass moved out from under the skiff, a huge, quivering shadow circling around below us like a submarine.

"Put the pole by my foot," Deeps said, the cable giving slightly. I moved the powerhead closer. Keo would've let me drive the Jeep for a month to have been here instead of me. Sweat started to bead on Deeps's head. He pulled the shark another foot closer.

"You're not going to shoot him *now*, are you?" I asked.

"No worry—just give me the pole when I tell you."

"But that thing's bigger than the *skiff*," I said.

Deeps wound the cable around one hand and pulled, then around the other. "I said no worry."

I dug my fingers into the wooden seat. I wanted to pace, I wanted to feel the concrete of the pier under my feet. I could see the shark's eyes.

I stopped breathing.

Deeps pulled the shark closer, never taking his eyes off it. Uncle Raz may have been right about Deeps knowing what he was doing, but Uncle Raz was sitting on the pier, and so were Dad and Keo.

A small whirlpool sucked at the side of the skiff as the shark's tail swung by in a sudden burst. A few feet of cable hummed out over the wooden gunwale. Deeps grabbed at it, and slowed the shark's run. Maybe it didn't even know it was hooked.

Dizziness overwhelmed me, a quivering sensation that ran across my forehead, and turned my stomach hot. Fear had struck me many times before, but never like this—the kind Deeps's dogs could smell. I saw the dream shark again, blasting up at me, at the yapping dog.

"Wait!" I yelled. "You can't take a chance on killing it in a boat this small. It's too *big*."

Deeps snapped around and glared at me, about to say something, but turned away, back to the shark, still holding the cable taut. He pulled the shark closer.

"*What if you miss?* Or what if you hit him right but he doesn't die? He could turn this thing over with one hit!" My whole body was shaking.

But all Deeps wanted was the shark. He stared at me through slits where eyes should have been. "Get hold of yourself, boy. I don't miss."

"But what if you do?"

"God*damn* it! *Shet!*" Deeps threw the cable back in the water. "Take me back to the pier."

I started the engine and moved us away quickly. Deeps turned his back to me as I wove the skiff through the buoys in the bay, my legs trembling.

A solemn conference of fishermen began as soon as we got out of the skiff. Deeps stood among them. They had to get a bigger boat for the shark.

I waited off to the side.

Keo came over. "What happened out there?"

"Nothing. The shark was too big for the skiff."

"It looked like you were yelling at each other."

"It was big. We got excited about it."

Keo shook his head. "I didn't think Deeps was such a pantie."

I shrugged. "It was too big, that's all."

Keo spit and walked away.

What was I going to do if Deeps wanted me to take him back out in the skiff?

The conference broke up and Uncle Raz walked over. "Come on," he said. "We're going to use my boat." He called to Keo. "You boys are going to see something today. Deeps says the bugger's a three-man fish."

Soon Uncle Raz was walking the *Optimystic* gently out to the buoy. Keo and I lay on the bow, hanging over the edge, searching the water. Usually we stood, but this time we weren't taking any chances. When we got to the buoy, we climbed up on the roof of the cabin. Dad and Uncle Harley waited on the after-deck, with Uncle Raz still at the wheel of the idling boat.

Deeps put a shotgun shell into the end of his aluminum powerhead. "Okay," he said. "Pull 'um up easy."

Uncle Harley fished the cable out from under the buoy.

Dad stood by with the gaff, a huge barbed hook on the end of a four-foot staff.

Uncle Harley pulled in on the cable, looping the line only once around each fist in case the shark took off and he had to let go quickly. The shark paced upward, a lethargic gray mass that disappeared under the boat, then reappeared, back and forth, growing larger as it rose to the surface.

"Hold steady," Deeps said. "I got to hit 'um just right. If I miss the spot, he's gonna go bananas."

Deeps held the powerhead with both hands, pointing it down into the water like a spear, waiting. When the shark's head appeared from under the boat, he struck down, jabbing the powerhead behind the eyes. The shark turned just as it hit.

The charge exploded, muffled by the water. White foam erupted off the stern, soaking Dad, Uncle Harley, and Deeps. The wounded shark hit the hull of the boat, sending a vibrating *thunnnck* through my body. The tiger's huge head rolled over, dark eye passing, massive cavernous mouth jarred open, blood pouring from the foot-wide mass of pulp where the powerhead had torn into the skin above his gills, a foot off the spine.

"Damn!" Deeps said.

Uncle Harley threw the cable out and moved back from the transom. The shark sank in a bubbling confusion of red, green, and white, water whirlpooling down into the spot where it had been.

Deeps thrashed through his bucket for a fresh charge and reloaded the powerhead, then went back to the transom. "Let 'um get used to the wound, then we pull 'um up again." He took two steps to the port side, then turned and paced back, checking the water around the buoy, swearing.

We waited about ten minutes, then Dad gaffed the cable and Uncle Harley started pulling the shark back up again, now having to work harder for it. The tiger resisted, but moved slowly upward, and Uncle Harley was able to get it back to the boat.

Again Deeps waited with the powerhead out over the water, taking his time. Uncle Harley was as tight as a rock trying to keep the shark within reach.

Deeps jabbed the powerhead down again. The back of the shark arched as the charge exploded, the thrashing tail sending a wash of red water into the boat, reaching even Keo and me on the roof. Dad leaned out over the transom and hooked the gaff into the shark's flank, just behind the eye. The muscles in Dad's glistening bare back stood out in ropelike bumps as he gripped the shaft and tried to keep the shark from shaking it out of his hands.

The shark slowly went limp, jerking in feeble spurts, sinking back into the bloody water, into the cloud of pulverized flesh that broke away and drifted off its back like silt.

"Got 'um! Broke the spine!" Deeps said, like a kid. He threw the powerhead onto the deck and grabbed the cable out of Uncle Harley's hands. With Dad and Uncle Harley's help, he dragged the dying shark closer to the boat and secured it to the stern.

Uncle Raz looped the *Optimystic* around slowly. A crowd of people started cheering as we approached the pier. Uncle Raz smiled and waved at them, and held his fist up in the air.

Deeps jumped off the boat and went to swing the fish hoist out over the water. Uncle Raz put the boat into neutral and let it idle while Keo jumped to the pier and secured the bow. I threw him the stern line.

Deeps dropped the huge hook down to the water. Dad and

Uncle Harley threw a cable loop around the tail of the tiger shark, and Deeps slowly pulled it out of the water.

The crowd went silent, then broke into amazed murmurs as it emerged.

It measured out at thirteen feet, four inches, and weighed 1,186 pounds. It was so long that we had to hang it out over the water. Deeps gaffed its head and together with four men lifted its nose up over the lip of the pier and laid it out on the concrete.

People crowded in as Deeps cut into the stomach. The place fell dead silent when he reached in and pulled out a whole turtle, not yet digested.

Then, working quickly, as if worrying that someone else might claim his trophy, Deeps cut into the shark's head, going after the jaw and teeth.

Keo squatted next to him and pulled the flesh away as Deeps carved into it. Soon Keo's hands were covered with blood and scraps of meat.

After Deeps had hacked the teeth free, Keo and Uncle Raz shoveled the guts into a fifty-gallon drum, then cut up and removed the shark in sections. Uncle Harley backed his truck up to haul away the meat.

Keo came up to me after Uncle Harley had driven off with the shark. "Want to come with me to take Deeps home? You can drive the first half," he said, dangling the keys in front of me.

I'd had enough of Deeps. But . . . "Okay." I reached for the keys.

Keo snapped them into his fist.

"First, I want to know what went on with you and Deeps in the skiff. I know what I saw, and you're not telling me everything. You got scared, didn't you?"

Just then, Deeps walked up and stood next to Keo, holding the shark's jaw. Keo flinched and stepped aside.

Deeps looked at me and lifted the jaw, tapping it with a

finger. "This guy," he said, "probably never would have hurt anyone . . . lazy things. But you never can tell—you never can tell."

I looked down at the fleshy bone, the knifelike teeth.

"You know the shark I was telling you about," he went on, "the one that ate the Hawaiian guy? Scared the piss out of me." He touched the jaw again. "Look nice when it's clean." He was so close I could see tiny specs of dried blood on his arm.

He handed me the jaw, holding it at the joint, away from the teeth. "Leave it out," he said. "Mongoose clean off the meat. Then bleach 'um in the sun, bombye come nice."

The jaw was heavy with seven rows of razor teeth, the bone slick with dangling cartilage.

"Let's go," Deeps said to Keo.

Keo was staring at the shark jaw, and jumped when Deeps spoke.

"Sure," Keo said.

He started toward the Jeep, then stopped and squinted at me. "You crack 'um up, you pay," he said, and threw the keys on the ground by my feet.

10

Rudy's Girl

(1965)

Until high school the harbor, the village, ten to
fifteen miles of coast, and the sea made up my
world.

I'd seen the island a thousand times from the
sea, fishing with Dad, a bluish mass of earth,
crowned with clouds and dotted with rooftops
high on the jungled rise of its steep flanks. The
rest of Hawaii could just as well have been
Zanzibar, for all I'd really known of it.

The high school was deep in the upper midlands, a half-hour ride on a crowded school
bus, and worlds away from the sea. Life was
different up there, not easy like down in the
village. It was tough if you managed to get on
the wrong side of someone. And to make things
worse, I was a white fishboy punk from down
by the ocean, which to some was worse than
being from California. Most people, though,
just minded their own business.

But then, there was Rudy Batakan.

We were in the same grade, though we'd
never spoken to each other until one day far
into our junior year. I was out on the football

field with a couple of friends during a class break. Rudy and four other guys walked up to us with their greased-back hair and bell-bottomed pants billowing out around their ankles so far you couldn't see their feet.

Rudy looked me over. "Eh, you stink like one fish. You one fish or what?" he asked in the pidgin English he spoke, *fish* coming out like *feesh*. Then he smiled, which threw me off. Was he clowning around or trying to start something?

"Barracuda," I said, hoping he was joking.

Rudy smirked. "Lissen, sissy punk," he said, jabbing me in the chest with his finger. "The new *baole* girl—don't mess wit' her." He glared at me, then smiled, a mean smile. "You mess wit' her, I mess wit' you."

One of his friends snickered. "Eh, Rudy. No scare him so much he make shee-shee pants." Everyone but Rudy laughed.

Rudy's face was less than a foot from mine, so close I could smell his hair grease. He poked me again, but not as hard. "No forget, eh?" he said, then strolled off with his pack.

I didn't even know the new girl's name. I'd seen her around, and once said hello to her. That's all.

From then on Rudy made a point of noticing me, always saying things like, "Eh, *baole* punk, howzit?" I wanted to say, "Fine, *manong* punk," *manong* being an unfriendly word for Filipino.

One morning before school Rudy passed by Keo and me and said, "Howzit, shee-shee pants." As always, a couple of guys were with him.

Keo snapped around. "Who you calling shee-shee pants?"

Rudy stopped, stunned. He glared at me, then at Keo. "Who said that?"

Keo stepped closer to Rudy. "I did."

Rudy's friends moved up beside him. "I calling that punk one fah-king *baole* shee-shee pants," he said. "What'choo care?"

"If he's one fah-king *baole* shee-shee pants, then you one fah-king *manong* shee-shee pants," Keo said, mimicking the way Rudy spoke.

"Wait," I said. "It's okay." I put my hand on Keo's shoulder, but he shrugged it away.

Rudy nosed up to Keo and pushed him back with his palms, his friends closing in behind.

Keo slugged him in the face.

Rudy reeled back and covered his nose with both hands. "You broke my nose!" he yelled, bent over. Tears flooded the edges of his eyes.

Two of his army made a move toward us but held off when a friend of Keo's stepped in.

I grabbed Keo's arm. "Let's get out of here."

He let me pull him away, but kept his eyes on Rudy's friends. Rudy broke through the crowd and headed into the building, a bloody hand over his nose.

He stayed away from school for a week after that, and when he returned the skin around his eyes was yellowy-purple.

Keo gave me a golf ball and told me to keep it with me at all times and squeeze it until my arm ached, then rest and start squeezing again. It would put muscle into my punch. He also told me to practice slamming the side of my fist into my stomach to make it hard. "You can't trust a punk like Rudy," Keo said. "Especially when he thinks you're fooling around with his girlfriend."

"But I don't even know her."

"Doesn't matter. Rudy thinks you do."

I kept away from Rudy until the school year ended. He was like one of those dogs that stand perfectly still as you approach, watching you, and if you look them in the eye they snap and go crazy.

*   *   *

That summer between my junior and senior year, I got a job running a small, thatch-roofed, glass-bottomed · catamaran, which I kept in a corner of the cove next to the pier.

Keo was on his own now, out of high school. He went to work as Uncle Raz's deckhand. He and Cheryl Otani were still going strong and were talking about getting married. Keo planned to get a boat like Uncle Raz's and fish for marlin.

Dad wanted me to work with him on the *Ipo*, fishing the tuna grounds. But I couldn't see spending day after day roasting on a hot boat in the middle of the ocean. I wanted to stay near town, near people. But I told Dad I wanted the glass-bottom boat job so I could learn the names of all the fish I didn't know. Dad said that was a good idea, and went on with his routine alone.

The glass-bottom boat business ran smoothly until the paddlers came.

I'd been keeping the cat beached in the cove at night, and stowing its ten-horse outboard in a storage room at King Kam Hotel. The sand on the small, white, half-moon beach was so fine it ran through your fingers like dream dust. Most of the time nothing much happened there beyond the noisy chatter of small kids splashing in the shallows and the occasional beaching of a skiff. In the mornings, I hammered a sign into the sand next to the boat: "Hawaiian Glass-Bottom boat rides, $5.00 per person, per hour," then sat around squeezing the golf ball and punching my stomach until someone wanted to go out.

Late one afternoon I came in from a two-hour tour down the coast with three ladies from England. When we puttered back into the cove, the paddlers were spread out over the beach, sitting in small groups and milling around the palm trees, forty or fifty canoe club kids waiting for practice to start.

After I ran the cat up onto the sand, the ladies got out and went off toward the pier. I straightened up the boat and watched the paddlers out of the corner of my eye. I knew most of them from school, though not very well. Many lived in the highlands and didn't spend much time down in the village.

I grabbed the sponge and bucket out of the stern and headed over for some fresh water.

Off to my left I noticed a small group of older paddlers sitting in the dappled shade of a clump of palm trees, four boys and two girls. One of the girls was blond, her hair tied back in a pony tail, white plumerias floating in the gold just above her left ear—the new girl. And next to her, Rudy.

He glared down at me, the sleeves on his white T-shirt rolled up to show off his homemade tattoo. "What'choo looking at, fishboy?"

I kept walking toward the hotel.

"Eh! Punk! I talking to you. What'choo looking at, I said?"

I stopped and turned. The new girl looked away as if embarrassed. But the rest of them gave me pretty solid stink eye.

"Me? I'm just going to get some fresh water." Rudy the creep playing King of the Beach.

"No lie, you fahkah," he said.

"Sorry," I said, not knowing what else to say.

"Sorry," Rudy mimicked. His friends got a pretty big kick out of it.

I walked away.

The paddling coach arrived and the kids swarmed over to the canoes and carried them gently down to the water. I filled the bucket and started back to the cat to wash the salt off the seats. How was I going to share the beach with Rudy for the next couple of months?

One afternoon about two weeks after the paddlers had shown up, I was drifting with a man and two old ladies in the cat, just outside the entrance to Thurston's Harbor, a man-made lagoon carved out of the rocky shoreline, sinking back into a mysterious private estate.

"See that fish just above the cauliflower coral," I said to the ladies. They were great, kept saying, "Yes, oh yes, I see," and "Isn't that nice." The man mostly sat there nodding with his arms crossed.

"That's called a *kikakapunukunukuoioi*," I said, knowing that I would impress them with a name that took me nearly a week to master.

And then a body appeared below the glass—long waving blond hair undulating outward, like delicate strings of sea grass.

The new girl.

"Oh my . . ." one of the ladies said, "a mermaid." The man unfolded his arms and bent in over the box.

The girl dove to the bottom and found a red sea star, then brought it up to us under the glass. She wore no face mask, but looked up with her eyes open, small bubbles of air escaping from the edge of her mouth. Loose strands of hair moved across her face, and billowed outward as she rose and hung below us.

Then she laughed, letting out a blast of bubbles that stuck to the bottom of the glass. When they cleared, she was gone. She popped up a few yards off the stern, waved, and swam toward the rocky shore.

"Is that your girlfriend?" one of the ladies asked.

"No," I said. "I've seen her around, but I don't know her."

"Well," she said, "it looks as if she's trying to tell you something."

The ladies giggled.

I shook my head. "Naah . . . naah."

But from then on there was hardly a minute in my life that wasn't filled with the memory of her smiling face looking up at me under the glass-bottom boat. I had it pretty bad, like I did with Melanie McNeil when I practically camped out at the post office waiting for letters that would never come. Feelings just rose up on their own, feelings that made my whole world seem different—brighter—*much* brighter. I began to hate weekends, when no paddlers came to the cove, when I had to spend two days straight without a chance to catch a glimpse of the one I now called Rudy's girl.

Was she Rudy's girl?

I saw her standing next to a canoe one day, getting ready to go out with the girls crew. I slowed the cat to a crawl and crept slowly into the cove and up to the beach, coming as close to the canoe as I dared, risking a warning from the coach.

"Hi," I said to her as I passed. She smiled and looked right at me, into my eyes.

When she came back from the practice run, she waded by the cat, wavelets arrowing out from her knees. She bunched her wet T-shirt at the bottom and squeezed the water from it. I was sitting in the boat under the thatch roof, one foot in the water and the other propped up on the rim of the glass box, listening to a transistor radio. I was feeling pretty good.

She threw her hair back and rolled it up like a towel on the side of her head—a luxurious gesture. She came up to the cat and stood playing with her hair, though for only a moment. Her eyes darted up toward Rudy, then back to me.

"Meet me here Friday night at seven-thirty," she said in a low voice, almost whispering. She looked into my eyes.

Just then, Rudy shouted. "Eh, Shelley, come on."

She looked down quickly and walked on past me. I kept my eyes on the water where she'd been standing.

My heart felt as if it would thump right out of my chest, her words pounding through my mind, "meet me, meet me, meet me . . ."

I tried to keep my gaze away from Rudy and the girl for the rest of that afternoon, cleaning the already clean boat.

Near the end of paddling practice Rudy walked into the water near the cat and sank down up to his neck. He moved around so he was facing me, and stared until I couldn't stand it. I took my radio and my golf ball out of the bucket and walked the arc of the beach over to the pier to watch the charter boats come in.

Keo was already back, the *Optimystic* lounging against the bumpers. "How's the beach bum business," he said, spraying fresh water over the stern deck.

"Pretty good. Except for Rudy Batakan—remember the guy you busted in the nose?"

Keo smirked. "How could I forget? What's he doing around here?"

"Paddling. But get this: you know the blond girl that hangs around with him? She's paddling, too. And that's not all—she came by the cat and whispered to me. Meet me on the pier Friday night, she said."

Keo raised his eyebrows. "You sly eel. You're asking for it, aren't you?"

"What do you mean, me? It was *her* idea."

"If I was in your ugly shoes," Keo said, then paused. He punched me in the arm. "I'd do it."

Waiting the three days for Friday to roll around was maddening. I even cut five or ten minutes off my charters. I wanted to be near her, to watch her walk down the beach, or sit pulling water in a canoe tied to shore, or see her sink down into the ocean after a workout and walk up the sand with her shirt stuck to her body.

When Friday night finally arrived I was as jumpy as a dog that knew he was going hunting. By seven-thirty the sky had darkened and had lost its brilliant sundown reds. I stood in the shadow of a palm tree, away from the burning torches lining the beach and hotel grounds, and studied every human movement for as far as I could see. The pier was quiet, as was the beach in the cove.

"Hi," someone said from behind me, nearly sending me out of my skin. Rudy's girl, wearing thongs, faded jeans with holes in the knees, and a light blue work shirt tied at her waist. Her hair hung over her shoulders looking yellow-silver in the flickering reflection of the torches.

"I'm glad you came," she said. "I was worried you wouldn't."

"Why?"

"Because of Rudy."

"Sorry to say this," I said, "but he's a jerk if there ever was one."

"Yeah."

"So your name is Shelley."

"How'd you know?"

"Rudy called you from the beach."

"And you're Sonny Mendoza," she said, smiling in the dim light. "I've been asking around."

I glanced over her shoulder. The top of a car crept toward the pier on the other side of the seawall. "Let's get out of here. Makes me nervous, fooling around with Rudy's girl."

She dropped her smile. "I'm not Rudy's girl, or anyone's girl."

"Tell Rudy that."

She frowned. "Come on. This makes me nervous, too."

We walked quickly around the cove and out toward the rocky point across from the end of the pier. We picked our way through the bushes and sat out on the round boulders, just a foot or two above the splash of waves. I could smell her perfume, she was so close.

I picked pebbles from between the boulders and threw them out into the black water. But Shelley wasn't so shy about talking.

She was from Chicago. Her parents had some buildings there and had made a lot of money, so they decided to move to the islands and retire early. Her father had a small plane and was thinking about starting an air-taxi business, taking people and cargo back and forth to Honolulu. Shelley was seventeen. My outlook for the future soared when it hit me that we'd be spending our senior year together.

I finally got up some nerve. "Why do you hang around with a guy like Rudy?"

"He's the first guy I met here," she said. "He was sitting with Jimmy and Lenny on the hood of Lenny's car in the school parking lot."

I nodded.

"Rudy scares me," she went on. "I don't know how to get away from him. He thinks he owns me."

I threw another pebble. "He thinks he owns the whole island. I've managed to keep clear of him—until now, anyway."

Shelley was quiet a moment, her face barely visible in the light from the pier. "I'm sorry, Sonny. It's my fault. Back when I first saw you at school, I asked Rudy who you were. He wouldn't tell me. I didn't know it would set him off like that."

"Aw, that's all right. If it wasn't me it would have been someone else."

A car pulled out onto the end of the pier. Its headlights shot out over the bay, then flooded the rocks.

"Duck," I whispered. We hunkered down into the crevices between the larger boulders as everything around us lit up.

Three people got out of the car and stood talking in front of the headlights, shadows flickering over us as they moved. They got back into the car and slowly circled around before leaving the pier.

"Ten bucks that was Rudy," I said. "We'd better get out of here. Let's sneak into Thurston's place, there, over the rock wall. It's private property, but they're not always around."

We climbed the wall and peered down into the estate. The house on the grounds was small. The man-made harbor was solid black and quiet. It circled around in front of the unlit house, then opened into a larger lagoon beyond.

"Someone could be sitting on the porch, in the shadows," I whispered. "There's probably no one there, but I can't tell for sure. We better go somewhere else."

Shelley touched my arm. "Let's *swim* in," she said. "Into the harbor."

I looked at her to see if she was joking. She wasn't. Sure. It was a great idea. We could swim past the house, climb up into the grounds from the harbor, and sneak on out to the beach on the far side of the estate. We'd be completely alone there.

Shelley climbed back down to the boulders below. By the time I caught up with her she'd untied the tails of her shirt and let them hang to her knees. She kicked her thongs away and took her jeans off, then stuck them under a stone. Her shirt looked like a short dress.

"Come on," she said, crouching on a large, flat rock and inching her way down into the water.

My God, she took off her jeans! A scorpion couldn't have gotten more attention out of me. She pushed off into the ocean, its blackness swallowing her.

I left my shorts on, but slipped my T-shirt off and stuck it under the stone with her jeans.

The ocean was warm. We swam slowly, searching the high sides of the entrance for movement. The water in Thurston's Harbor was still and much colder than the open sea. Fresh water springs bubbled up under us and spread outward on the surface. Shelley swam close to me, our arms bumping, her breathing quick.

She followed me to a rock stairway that climbed up out of the water onto a series of terraces that rose from the lagoon. Soundlessly we made our way to a grassy area bound by a low rock wall lined with palm trees. And beyond, the ocean.

We dropped over the wall and lay on our backs in the sand. A zillion stars spread over us, the Milky Way trailing from one horizon to the other, a wispy white mist.

"You know, Sonny," Shelley said. "For the first time since I came to Kona I feel as if I could close my eyes and not have to worry about a thing. I hardly even know you, but it doesn't seem to matter. I even felt it before I knew who you were, when I first saw you at school. How come?"

"Don't ask me," I said, "I'm having a hard enough time just keeping *up* with you."

And I was. It was impossible for me to think of anything else but her.

From there it got worse.

The next three weeks went by as if I lived in a dream. It didn't even feel like the same world, let alone the same village. *Everything* I did had some part of Shelley tied into it.

Whenever we could manage it, we met at night and swam into Thurston's Harbor. We spent hours lying side by side on the sand, holding hands and staring up at the stars. When the full moon came, the night sky seemed to explode, a brilliant, silvery-gray illumination as deep as the relentless, almost painful feelings that drove me. We spent hours wrapped around each other, kissing, as if kissing were the sweetest of life's gifts.

Once, Shelley turned on her side and rested her head on my shoulder, her damp hair pressing up against my cheek. I ran my fingertips over the smooth skin of her face, and a pure, euphoric feeling raced through me. The life I'd lived until then seemed so far away, faint as a whisper, insignificant. At home I looked at Dad and wondered if it had been that way for him, if my mother had whispered in his ear. I wondered if he'd really known her the way I knew Shelley.

Every night Shelley asked me what it was that made her want to be with me at every hour of every day. And always I felt a knot clumping up in my throat and answered with a shrug. We talked of spending our last year in high school together, then maybe going to college in Honolulu, or getting jobs in the village.

Dad couldn't help but notice that I was spending so much time out at night. One afternoon at the pier I said, "See that blond girl over there under the coconut trees?"

Dad squinted across the cove. Shelley was sitting with Rudy and two other guys. None of them noticed us. Dad nodded.

"That's Shelley . . . my girlfriend."

"Then what's she doing with those guys?"

"It's a long story."

Dad raised an eyebrow, then gave me his entire lesson on sex education. "Watch out you don't knock anyone up," he said. Then he smiled and walked over to his Jeep.

Rudy had been watching me lately. And though Shelley had been nearly invisible in getting to the cove on the nights we met, both of us felt the constant threat of being surprised. Shelley still sat on the beach with Rudy, because she was afraid of what he might do if he ever found out that we'd been together. He'd asked her a hundred times to go places with him and his friends, in Lenny's primer-gray, low-riding Chevy, but she'd always refused, telling him her father didn't allow her to date.

Nothing in my life had ever had made my stomach roll as much as seeing the two of them sitting together under the palms when I came in from a charter.

One moonless night when Shelley and I were on the beach out at Thurston's, we heard voices coming from the blackness behind us in the palm trees. Shelley dug down into the sand, trying to disappear.

I turned over slowly onto my stomach and looked toward the trees. "Don't move," I whispered. We were close enough to an outcropping of lava that our bodies, held perfectly still, could be taken for part of the rocky shoreline.

There was no mistaking the sound of Rudy's voice. "They out here somewhere—I going kill the fahkah."

"How you know dat, brah? Maybe was someone else you saw."

"Was dem, I tell you."

Shelley dug her fingers into my arm and tried to inch closer to the rocks. But we had to lie still.

A cigarette glowed bright orange, then shot out over the wall, flipping sparks as it twirled toward the ocean. Behind us waves rolled in a continuous rush over the jagged rocks and into the tidal pools just inches beyond our feet.

One of the shadows dropped down to the sand. I had to fight the urge to grab Shelley and run for it. We *could* make it, I thought. We could hide. With a decent head start we could make it.

The shadow walked around on the sand, then started back up toward the wall. Then he stopped and seemed to be staring at the spot where we lay. He took a step closer and bent forward.

"Get ready to run for it," I whispered. "One more step and he'll see us."

But then the shadow turned away and went back to the wall. The four shapes moved together and spoke in a low murmur, then separated, spreading out along the length of the wall above us, blocking any chance of a run for the trees.

"They know we're here," I whispered to Shelley. "They've blocked us off. We can let them get us, or we can swim."

Shelley's body shook, pressing up against me. "Follow me as

closely as you can," I said. "It's not going to be easy getting over the rocks.

"Now!"

I pulled her by the hand. Tidal pools were everywhere, knee-deep and covered with submerged hooks and knives of rock and coral. Sometimes we had to crawl, feeling our way into the blackness. The only consolation was in knowing that Rudy had to face the same problem.

They shouted behind us. "There! There! They heading for the water! Get 'um!"

My feet were tough, but Shelley cried as she stumbled over the sharp lava. By the time we finally reached the ocean, her sobs quivered out in frantic whimpers, more from fear than pain.

As we swam away, I looked back. Like hunters tracking a pig, the four shadows moved along the rocks. We couldn't have been more than two nearly invisible dots among a million black and gray flickers of moving ocean. Finally they gave up and disappeared into the trees.

We swam in past the pier and across the harbor, so we could get out of the water at the cove in front of the palace. Rudy would probably be hanging around the pier watching for us.

When we finally dragged ourselves out of the water, barely having the strength to crawl, Shelley sat close to me, shivering on the sand.

"Let's get up into the trees," she said, too scared and too tired to push her tangled wet hair out of her face. "He knows it was us."

"Maybe," I said.

"I'm afraid, Sonny. Rudy gets crazy. I just want to get away, but I can't. And now I've got you dragged into it."

"I dragged myself in. Stop worrying, we'll think of something."

I wondered just what in the world I had in mind to do. I didn't have the guts to tell Shelley that I was just as scared of

Rudy and his gang as she was. He might slap her around a little, but I didn't think he'd lose any sleep over slitting my belly with a switchblade, with an extra slice for what Keo had done to him at school.

We walked along the road out of town to Shelley's house, ducking into the bushes whenever a car approached. Shelley limped most of the way, her feet cut up pretty badly. I tied palm fronds around them to ease the pain.

When we finally got there she stood with her arms around my neck and hugged me a long time, hanging on as if it would be the last time we'd ever see each other. I closed my eyes and slid helplessly into the blissful trance of closeness.

A light went off in her house. I pulled away. I hadn't even met her parents yet. They'd always been asleep by the time we'd walked home. I didn't want them to see Shelley with cut feet and tangled hair and wonder what I did to her. And worse, her jeans were still stuck under a rock at the cove.

"Be careful," Shelley whispered as I moved away into the darkness. "I'd die if anything happened to you."

I walked the mile more down the coast to my house, the dream of Shelley flickering, a slow-building dread gnawing at me.

The dogs trotted out to me. I knelt down and scratched their ears and let them lick my face. The light from the kitchen window flickered in their eyes.

When I stood, they spread out and returned to their sleeping spots, one of them leading me up the steps to the porch. Popoki sat at the top. She pretty much ran the place. She stood and stretched when I whispered her name.

Dad was sitting at the kitchen table with a small pile of papers and his checkbook, a cup of coffee steaming near his right hand. His wavy hair curled around his ears. Streaks of gray were beginning to mar the deep brown above his forehead.

In his thick, callused fingers the thin ballpoint pen looked out of place.

I sat down across from him, still damp and itching from the drying salt.

Dad leaned back in his chair and crossed his arms. "You've been pretty busy lately," he said.

I nodded, and said, "Busy's too slow a word."

He smiled. "What's going on?"

I hadn't realized how much I'd been keeping to myself since I'd met Shelley. It all started pouring out. I told him about the paddlers and Rudy and Shelley, then what had happened down at Thurston's. "It's like I'm going crazy or something. She's all I can think of anymore. But Rudy. What do I do about him?"

Dad sat back, thinking, staring at the table.

"I wish my mother were here," I said, then suddenly realized what I'd said.

Dad looked up.

". . . I mean . . . maybe she would have understood about Shelley and Rudy."

Dad stared at his hands, playing with the pen. He always seemed to know about people like Rudy, about how they think, and how to deal with them. But Shelley. Could he even guess at what she might be feeling?

"She probably would have," he finally said. "She was like your Aunty Pearl. She had a big heart."

Dad frowned. "Do you think this girl has been leading Rudy on, and maybe you?"

"No," I said, his words cutting me. "She's not like that. She's new here and just got mixed up with him because she didn't know anyone, that's all."

Dad stared at me. "It seems pretty clear to me, son. You can live in fear of this boy or meet him face to face. If you want to be with her, there's not much else you can do."

"I know," I said. I knew it the minute I started liking Shelley.

I went outside and took off my clothes. The dogs sat watching while I hosed the salt off my body. The night air was warm, and the rubbery taste of hose-water gave me a moment of peace. I was at home, with Dad and the dogs, and Popoki the queen, safe, for the moment, from even my own mind.

The next day when I came in with the glass-bottom boat, a crew of boy paddlers stood waist-deep in the water by a canoe. Rudy lounged under the trees, his arm hanging loosely around Shelley's neck. As the cat glided up to the sand, Shelley glanced down at me, but quickly turned away. Her knees were drawn up to her chin, and her arms wrapped around her legs.

"Eh! Shee-shee pants," Rudy called to me.

I ignored him and started cleaning up the boat.

"Eh, I talking to you." He jumped to his feet along with two of his friends.

A wave of fear ran through me.

On the other side of the cove Dad was just sitting down on the wood rail that ran along the edge of the pier. He must have cut his fishing day short. He peered down into the water, as if watching for crabs. He never looked directly at me, but I knew why he was there.

I turned toward Rudy, but ignored him. "Shelley," I said.

Her mouth opened slightly, as if she thought I'd gone clean out of my head. Then her eyes dropped.

Rudy stepped between us, blocking her from view. The muscles in his jaw rippled as he glared at me.

I walked closer, starting around Rudy, and reached out my hand. "Shelley, come with me."

Rudy slammed his hands against my chest, pushing me backward toward the cat. His two friends moved to each side of me, just out of reach.

Rudy grabbed my T-shirt, but I knocked his hand away with

my arm. One of his friends circled around and grabbed me from behind. Rudy raised his fist, but held back when his friend suddenly backed off and tipped his head over toward the pier where Dad stood with his arms crossed, staring over at us.

"You're dead meat," he said, then flew at me.

"*Rudy stop!*" Shelley ran toward us. Rudy's friends grabbed her and held her back.

I fell backward when Rudy slammed into me, landing hard, rolling into the water. He jumped up quickly and sat on my stomach. Water washed over my eyes and into my mouth. He punched at my face in rapid jabs.

I heaved up with my stomach and rolled to the side, throwing him off. He swung as he fell, wildly, and I punched back. I dove at him, getting too close to swing. We wrestled in the water, gasping, each of us trying to drown the other. I must have swallowed a couple of gallons of salt.

I got one more punch in that made his mouth bleed. Then I felt hands on my shoulders. The coach stepped between us.

"Rudy! Get the hell out of here. You ain't paddlin' for me today!" The coach glared at him. The rest of the paddlers pressed in, a hundred eyes, waiting.

Rudy scrambled up, a little wobbly. He wiped his hand across his mouth, smearing the blood. I was on my knees trying to catch my breath when I saw him coming and fell to the side. He missed me completely and sprawled into the water. I jumped up with my fists clenched and backed off a couple of steps. The coach reached down and grabbed Rudy from behind, by the hair. Rudy got up on his knees. He whipped his arm back at the coach, thinking it was me. The coach surrounded Rudy's chest with his other arm and lifted him up. Rudy flailed back, but the coach held him until he stopped swinging.

"Go home and cool off." He let Rudy go.

"You dead, fahkah, you dead, you *dead*!" he spit at me, then glared at Shelley and stormed off toward town.

Over at the pier Dad strolled away toward the boats. I bent over with my hands on my knees, trying to catch my breath.

Rudy's friends let Shelley go and she ran into the water. She knelt next to me, crying. "I'm sorry, I'm sorry, it's all my fault . . ."

"It's okay . . ." I said between the gaps in my breathing. "It's okay . . ."

My face throbbed, and my legs felt weak. Inside, my heart pounded like racing pistons.

Shelley helped me pull the cat up on the sand and stake it down, then bathed my face with fresh water, waiting in silence for me to settle down.

We spent the rest of the afternoon alongside the pier on Dad's boat, together for the first time in open daylight. The ropes creaked as wide swells passed under the hull, lifting us, then dropping us down gently.

My face stung, but the sun felt as good as it ever had at anytime in my life.

"What happened to *you*?" Keo asked when I saw him the next day.

"Got in a fight with Rudy."

"For what?"

"Shelley."

"I hope it was worth it."

"I'd do it again if I had to."

I stayed jittery for the next couple of weeks, thinking Rudy would suddenly appear with two or three of his friends, especially somewhere along the road to my house where there were long stretches of nothing but grass, weeds, and trees.

Free of Rudy, Shelley was a new person. We went everywhere together, and at any time of day. I even met her parents.

"Sonny," her mother said, pausing, as if wanting to remember my name. "Nice to meet you." She had some kind of mainland accent. She shook my hand like a man would, with a strong grip, and pulled me into the house before letting go. "You look like you just walked out of an Edgar Rice Burroughs book," she said.

"Huh?"

"You know, Tarzan."

I liked her instantly.

Her father was an inch shorter and just as friendly. He had a thick blond mustache. *No* one I knew had a mustache. Uncle Raz said only pansies had them. But Shelley's father didn't seem like a pansy to me.

"You like machines?" he asked.

I shrugged. "I guess so."

"Good. Then you'll like what I've got in the garage."

I glanced at Shelley and she rolled her eyes, then smiled. We followed him out to the garage. Carefully, he pulled away a blue canvas tarp.

"Sweet, huh?"

I stared at the small black Alfa Romeo. It had a wooden dashboard and wooden steering wheel. I'd never seen anything like it.

From then on Shelley's father picked me up on the road whenever he found me walking home.

Shelley quit paddling, and stayed away from the cove until each practice was over. I tried to schedule my charters so that I'd be out most afternoons.

But before summer was over I ran into Rudy again.

The first time, Shelley and I had just finished putting the glass-bottom boat up for the day and were walking back through town on the island side of the road. We were holding hands and talking. Suddenly Shelley fell silent.

Rudy was slouching against a rock wall with four stone-faced boys, all of them staring at us. I felt the skin on the back of my neck start to crawl. But he said nothing as we hurried by.

The second time I was up the hill at the barber shop sitting on the bench outside with my eyes closed, waiting for Dad. The air was cool at that elevation. It was so quiet I could hear a car coming up the road four or five minutes before it passed by.

"Mendoza," someone said, standing to the side so the sun streamed into my eyes. It was the first time Rudy and I had ever met alone. He laughed and said, "No worry, *baole*. I no like fight."

"That makes two of us," I said, squinting up at him and shielding my eyes from the sun.

Rudy smirked. "The barber, my grandmother's cousin—the old buk-buk got me working his coffee."

I studied him. Rudy acting like a normal person? What was he getting at?

He nodded and started to leave. "No move when the old man uses the razor, eh? He getting pretty old." He laughed and went on down the road.

He seemed like a different person without his gang around. I could almost like him.

As the days rolled on, I could tell by the way Dad treated me that I'd climbed a notch in his eyes. And though Rudy had dragged my summer down, Shelley gave it wings, and light, and sky, and hope for the future. We worked the glass-bottom boat together, me running the boat, and she talking to tourists and leading them down to the cove, then diving for coral and shells, bringing them up under the glass and carefully replacing them for the next group.

I did two things the rest of that summer—learned almost all I know about shells, fish, and coral, and fell deeper and deeper and deeper under Shelley's spell.

11

Islanders
(1966)

Family.

I should have thought of a thousand things to say when Shelley asked me what mine was like. But all I said was, "It's just me and Dad. We're on our own, pretty much . . ."

That sounded so empty.

We were on the point off Thurston's Harbor watching the sun go down and talking about the future. Shelley wanted to study hotel management at the University of Hawaii in Honolulu. She wanted me to go there, too. Just the two of us, getting jobs and going to school together—living our own lives, like Aunty Pearl and Uncle Harley.

We sat side by side on the sand between the rocks, arms and knees touching. Could I even survive if I didn't go with her?

Shelley tapped me on my arm and pointed toward the lighthouse on the far point. A boat I'd never seen before was heading in toward the harbor—a yacht. Shelley leaned into my shoulder, and we watched it approach.

As it got closer I could tell by the way it cut

the water that it was easily the best-made boat I'd ever seen. A man stood at the wheel in a sunken cockpit, and a woman coiled a length of rope on the bow. The yacht sailed past, toward the harbor, silent as a cat's ghost. It said *Moineau, Papeete,* in gold script across its dark wood stern.

"Holey, moley," I whispered, then whistled softly.

"Sparrow," Shelley said. "What a beautiful name."

"Huh?"

"Sparrow, that's the name of the boat. *Moineau* is sparrow in French."

I nodded, half listening, mesmerized by the yacht's sharp, clean lines.

Sparrow. Pure, fluid. It fit.

I floated away, daydreaming. I was at the helm, sailing at my own speed to wherever I felt like going, the wheel smooth and steady in my hands. The yacht belonged to me and Shelley. Alone, we were sailing the oceans of the world.

Then, suddenly jolted in my daydream, I thought of Dad's sampan, only it was a dark, deserted ghost boat—a shadow chugging slowly away. It disappeared under the sharp, blue line that divided the sea from the sky.

Where did *that* come from?

I closed my eyes and shook the thought away, wiping my sweating hands on my T-shirt.

The *Moineau* anchored close in, bow to the sea, stern tied to the end of the pier. Shelley and I swam past its clean, white wooden hull on our way out of Thurston's Harbor. I ran my hand along its side at the waterline, felt its smoothness.

The man and woman worked side by side, furling the sails and stowing gear without speaking, as if they'd been sailing together forever. Neither of them looked much older than twenty or twenty-five. How could they be so young and have a boat like this?

The man stood a moment when he saw us watching him. He nodded, and I lifted my chin. Then he turned away and took a bucket up onto the pier.

We found Keo and Uncle Raz sitting in Uncle Raz's truck drinking beer, the two of them slouching in their seats with the doors open. When we walked up Uncle Raz waved his bottle toward the *Moineau*.

"Foo-foo, yeah?"

Keo smirked, then waved past Uncle Raz to Shelley.

"A boat like that," Uncle Raz went on, "is good for nothing but a tea party."

I turned and glanced back at the yacht. Uncle Raz never had taken to people who didn't work for a living, even people like Shelley's father who'd earned enough to retire while still pretty young. And he'd sooner get caught driving a pink Cadillac convertible than fiddling around on a cocky boat like the *Moineau*.

"I think it's kind of . . . beautiful," I said.

"*Beautiful!*" Uncle Raz pinched up his eyes and pulled his head back into his neck, then turned to Keo. "What is he? A fisherman or a macaroni?"

Keo peeked over at me and smiled. "Macaroni. No doubt about it."

"What's wrong with it?" Shelley asked.

Uncle Raz looked like he'd just licked a lemon. "What can you do with it? Can't fish. Can't take a lot of people anywhere. Can't even say the name. You can go for a boat ride, that's all."

Shelley held his gaze and Uncle Raz blinked. He could stare a man down for days, but Tutu Max had beaten him into learning about women a long time ago. He waved his beer toward me and said to Shelley without looking at her, "You go fishing with this boy's daddy and he'll show you what a boat is for."

"Where is he, anyway?" I asked Uncle Raz. "He should have been back an hour ago."

"Last I heard he was way down past Milolii."

I squinted into the sunset and scanned the horizon. No boats. Fishermen were funny sometimes—superstitious. And Dad was no different from the rest of them. Taking a female fishing was bad luck, like bananas. I wondered what he'd say about taking Shelley along. He didn't know her very well. He was nice to her, but he usually just nodded and went on with what he was doing. It didn't seem to bother Shelley.

"I'll ask him," Shelley said.

Uncle Raz smiled. "You not bad, girl. Got a little bit of boy inside you, I can see."

Shelley stuck her arm through mine and said, "Maybe . . . maybe."

Uncle Raz swung his beer again, his favorite pointer. He said to Shelley, "Maybe you can show Sonny some things, eh? Straighten him out about boats."

I pulled Shelley away. "Come on. It's embarrassing that I'm related to this babooze."

The sky had darkened by then, and the *Moineau*'s night lights stretched off its beam in long, wobbly reflections. For an instant it hit again, that eerie thought—Dad's boat, a ghost boat, sinking into the horizon.

I strode off quickly, dragging Shelley along behind me.

"What's wrong?" she asked. She stopped and made me look into her eyes. "*What?*"

"I don't know. Something doesn't feel right, that's all."

"Well, what does it feel like?"

I looked up into the black sky, my hands on my hips, and took a deep breath. ". . . Ghosts," I said.

Shelley giggled, then stopped. "I'm sorry, Sonny. Really. It just sounded funny the way you said it. What do you mean, ghosts?"

"I don't know . . . I guess I'm just worried about Dad. He should have been back by now."

Shelley wrapped herself around my arm and snuggled up close to me. It was a small gesture. But it melted me down like ice in the sun.

She stared at me a moment, then gave me a nudge. "Come on, you need to get yourself home for some hot soup and a good night's sleep. He'll show up."

I waited up most of the night, dozing at times, but fitfully. At five the next morning, I called Uncle Raz's house, but he didn't answer. Right after I hung up, the phone rang.

"Uncle Raz just called from the pier," Keo said. "Your dad's boat isn't there. Did he ever come home?"

"No."

Keo was silent a minute. Then he said, "We're on our way down to the pier. Start walking. We'll pick you up on the road."

I felt my hands sweating again. Where *was* he? Why didn't he radio in?

The dogs whined when I turned on the kitchen light, crowding around on the porch by the screen door as if they knew something wasn't right. I fed them and hurried out to the shadowy road. The sun was still far below the mountain, but the sky was beginning to turn an early-morning pale.

Keo and Uncle Harley picked me up a mile from town, the brightness of the Jeep's headlights dimming when Uncle Harley took his foot off the gas pedal. I climbed over the spare tire into the backseat.

"Tell me everything you know about where he might have gone yesterday," Uncle Harley said.

"I don't know anything," I said. "He just went out as usual. Where do you think he is?"

"Who knows? But he would have used the radio if he was in trouble."

"Maybe he ran out of gas."

"Maybe. But still he would radio."

No one said anything for a while. I glimpsed the ocean through the trees, gray and calm, the ghostly white of breaking waves flaring up below the palms. *What do you know?*

Nothing.

It surprised me to think that. And it scared me. I knew nothing about where Dad was. Did I even know much about *who* he was? Our lives went on. That's all.

When we drove out to the end of the pier, Uncle Raz was just pulling the *Optimystic* away from its mooring in the harbor, walking the boat in toward us. Dad's buoy was pale white against the flat sea. The skiff was still tied to it.

Keo and I jumped out of the Jeep and studied the ocean, straining to see a sign down the southern coastline, a light, a dark speck.

Uncle Harley pushed himself up and stood on the seat. He panned the horizon with a pair of binoculars. "Nothing," he said. "Only a sailboat."

I turned to where the *Moineau* had anchored the night before. It was gone.

Uncle Raz parked the boat and walked over. "I've been trying to call Raymond for the last hour, but he still doesn't answer."

"Or can't answer," Uncle Harley said. "What do you think?"

"Keep calling and go look," Uncle Raz said.

We decided that Keo and I would go with Uncle Raz on the boat, and Uncle Harley would drive down the coast checking the harbors. We'd search until three o'clock. If Dad hadn't shown up by then, we'd call the Coast Guard.

"Sonny," Uncle Harley said. "Think hard—did he say anything at all about where he was going yesterday?"

I shook my head.

Uncle Harley pressed his lips together, then said, "Okay, let's go."

"Sonny." Keo nodded down the pier. "Your girlfriend."

Shelley and her father drove up to us in the Alfa Romeo. Shelley got out.

"Did he come back?"

"No," I said. "We're going out to look for him now."

Shelley turned toward the car. "Daddy . . ."

Her father turned off the engine and got out. "Mick Pierce," he said, sticking his hand out to Uncle Harley, then to Uncle Raz. "Hi, boys," he said to Keo and me. Then he put his hand on my shoulder. "Shelley told me you were worried about your father."

Shelley watched me, eyes pinched with concern.

"We're all worried, Mr. Pierce," Uncle Harley said. "He didn't come back to the harbor last night, and we can't raise him on the radio."

"Call me Mick," he said, smiling. "I can help. I've got a little single-engine Cessna out at the airport."

Uncle Harley glanced over at Uncle Raz. Uncle Raz shrugged and said, "He'll cover a lot more water than I will."

Uncle Harley thought for a second. Then he looked Mr. Pierce in the eye. "We could use your help, Mick . . . it could be a wild goose chase, though. There's a lot of water out there."

Mr. Pierce nodded, his smile gone.

"You'll be looking for a blue and orange sampan," Uncle Harley added. "About thirty feet long. Open deck."

"I know the boat. Shelley pointed it out to me. I'll fly north and work my way south. We can keep in touch by radio." He called for Shelley as he started back to his car.

Shelley looked at Uncle Raz, not following.

"Why not," Uncle Raz said, cracking his sour expression. "Get on board."

Mr. Pierce nodded and drove off.

As we sped out of the harbor, the morning sun burst over the mountain, pouring color into the ocean. I stared out to sea with my knees braced against the gunwale. Shelley surrounded me with her arms from behind.

At ten minutes past ten, Mick Pierce's voice spat over the radio, his words broken by heavy static.

". . . the *Opti . . . stic*, callin . . . the *Op . . . ystic* . . ."

Uncle Raz grabbed the transmitter. "*Optimystic* back, over . . ."

"I foun . . . th . . . boat . . . about fifteen mil . . . northwest of . . . airport . . . I've circ . . . twice, but don't se . . . anyone aboard . . . she's running, though . . . head . . . away from the island, but slo . . . maybe . . . couple of knots, over . . ."

"He could be down in the hold," I said to Uncle Raz.

"Mick . . . can you see if the hold door is open? Look by the wheel, over . . ."

Continuous static rushed over the speaker. No one spoke.

"The door . . . open, but ther . . . sn't seem to be anyone in ther . . . from here . . . over."

Uncle Raz held the transmitter to his mouth but didn't say anything. Had Dad somehow fallen overboard?

"I'm on my way," Uncle Raz finally said. "Can you stay in the air until you see me coming . . . just long enough to give me a bead on the location? Over . . ."

"Roger . . . I can give y . . . twenty min . . . s, then I have t . . . back, over . . ."

"Hang on, Mick," Uncle Raz said. "*Optimystic* out."

Uncle Raz swung the boat around and blasted up to three thousand RPM. Still in the lee of the island, the ocean was smooth, and Uncle Raz's boat skimmed over it like a flying fish.

Mr. Pierce had located Dad's sampan miles from where he usually fished. Why? And the boat was under way with no one aboard. Was he sick? That was it, he was sick and sleeping in the hold out of the sun. Too sick to crawl out when he heard the plane.

Shelley put her hand on my chest. "Sonny . . ." she said softly.

"We'll find him," Uncle Raz said. "If we have to search from here to New Zealand, we'll find him."

Keo took Uncle Raz's binoculars up on the roof. He'd been quiet all morning. What would we find on the sampan? Would Dad be inside?

For the first time in my life I was afraid to climb aboard Dad's boat.

When Mr. Pierce spotted the *Optimystic* racing out toward Dad's boat, he called to tell us we were right on line. ". . . Still no sign of life . . ." he added. "Maybe he fe . . . overboard."

Uncle Raz answered slowly. "We'll take it from here, Mick . . . You alert the Coast Guard." Uncle Raz paused, then said, ". . . I'll buy you a beer when we get back . . . out."

". . . You're on."

Uncle Raz turned the static down. He didn't say anything. But I knew what he was thinking. If Dad was in the water, he was going to be hell to find.

Dad's sampan appeared and disappeared in the growing swells, slowly making headway to the northwest. Probably on auto pilot, Uncle Raz said. It was holding a steady course. Looking at it through the binoculars made me feel strange inside, hollow, like I wasn't really there but was dreaming about it.

We caught up around two-thirty. The deep-sea swells had risen noticeably, though the wind hadn't picked up.

"Keo," Uncle Raz called, sticking his head out the window and shouting to the roof.

Keo dropped onto the stern deck and came into the cabin.

"I'm going to pull up next to it," Uncle Raz said. "I'll ride alongside until you can jump over."

"I'm going with him," I said.

"No. I need you here."

"But . . ."

"Just wait a minute," Uncle Raz said.

Uncle Raz slowed the *Optimystic* and crept up to Dad's sampan. The swells were choppy, and Uncle Raz had to keep eight or ten feet away because the sampan could veer into us unexpectedly. There was always a good deal of play in an automatic pilot device.

The *Ipo* looked eerie as we rode along her port side. On deck, Dad's gaff slid one way and then the next with the movement of the hull, the pilotless steering wheel roaming around and back on its own.

The door to the hold stood open, slapping against the bulkhead. If Dad was on board, he was in there. My legs felt weak and started to shake.

Uncle Raz inched closer. The sampan's diesels *tok-tokked* over the quiet gas engines of the *Optimystic*, the exhaust gurgling from the pipes when the stern rose out of the water in a swell.

Keo stood on the gunwale holding onto the grabrail with one hand. Waiting. When both boats dropped into an easy trough between swells, he jumped.

Keo hit the deck behind the fish box and tumbled down against the gunwale on the other side of the boat. He jumped up quickly and made his way forward to the hold.

When he reached the controls he put the boat in neutral and glanced over at us. Uncle Raz nodded and Keo ducked down into the hold. Just a berth and a lot of junk—life jackets, emergency food, fishing gear. I could see it all as clearly as if I were there myself.

Keo scrambled out. "He's not there."

"Pull closer," I demanded.

Keo and I searched every inch of the boat for a sign, a clue. We found a seventy- or eighty-pound tuna in the fish box, and Dad's T-shirt on the deck near the wheel, but everything else was as it always was.

Except the net.

"The hand net is gone," I called over to Uncle Raz. Shelley watched from the gunwale, standing as Keo had before he jumped.

Uncle Raz frowned back at me.

"Check the gas," he called.

"It's okay," Keo yelled back a moment later.

"Sonny, jump back, and Keo, you bring the boat in to Kailua. Call Harley and tell him what's going on. Tell him we're going to stay out and search the water."

Keo put the sampan in gear and inched it closer to the *Optimystic*. "Jump when you're ready," he said. He stared at me as if he wanted to say more.

As the sampan pulled away, Keo almost looked like Dad. Scowling at the water like a fisherman. Standing at the wheel, swinging it around and finding his course. Balancing on the rocking deck like he'd been born there.

I watched the *Ipo* shrink away, no longer feeling sick, or worried. I was numb.

I even forgot about Shelley.

When the sky turned black we gave up and aimed in toward the harbor. Even in full daylight finding a man at sea was like trying to find a fishhook in the sand. At night it was impossible.

Keo radioed and said he was just off the lighthouse near Thurston's Harbor. He could see lights on the pier. "Something's going on, there," he said. There was a long pause. Then he added, "Sonny . . . Uncle Raymond is a good swimmer . . . if he fell off the boat, he could make it to shore . . ."

My jaw ached from jamming my teeth together. Making it

to shore was one thing. Sharks were another. And what if he hadn't fallen overboard? What if something *else* had happened? The vision of Dad's boat sinking below the horizon suddenly came back to me, then disappeared. Then the old dream-memory, the haunting unexplainable memory. *Don't ever do that again, boy! Never! Calm down, now . . . it was nothing . . .*

I stared into the black water. My throat began to burn. Shelley stood behind me, her arms around my stomach. I put my hands on hers, and could feel her head resting on my shoulder.

The village lights from the sea at night had always been warm and welcoming. But now they looked strange, almost foreign.

A group of fishermen mingled in the stale light falling from the fish hoist. Dad's sampan was tied alongside the pier. No one spoke as we docked behind it.

Uncle Harley jumped down onto the boat. "Anything?"

I shook my head.

Uncle Raz came aft, bags under his eyes. "Now what?"

"All these men will go out in the morning," Uncle Harley said, tilting his head toward the pier. "We'll cover a mile of coastline each, and zigzag out as far as we can go." He turned and glanced up at Shelley's father, who was waiting on the pier. "Mick will look from the air. And the Coast Guard is sending a search and rescue boat. It's on its way now."

Uncle Harley put his hand on my shoulder. "Come stay with us tonight, Sonny. We can't do any more until tomorrow."

I told him I had to go home first and feed the dogs, and that I'd be up later. I'd take Dad's Jeep. But what I really needed was time alone, to think.

"Can I ride with you?" Shelley asked.

I nodded and she followed me. When we got to the Jeep, I didn't want to get in. I started pacing back and forth, feeling sick again, thinking about Dad being alone in the ocean in the night, swimming—if he could, if he was alive—or sinking from exhaustion, lungs filling with water, gagging. *It's okay, boy. Calm down, now . . . You're not a baby anymore . . .* I was in the water, under water, breathing the sea, raking and clawing, trying to scream . . . something slammed into my back, ripped at my back . . .

"*Dad!*"

"Sonny," Shelley said, her eyes wide. "What is it?"

Then I remembered.

I *remembered*!

I must have been one or two years old. I was in the skiff with Dad, sitting up on the bow in a life vest that was too big for me. Dad was going fast, the boat bouncing. I leaned my face out over the water, feeling the air rush into my nose, feeling it run around me. Then we hit something, a chop, and I fell overboard. I went under the boat and was pounded in the back, pounded by the propeller, my life vest shredding. I tumbled around trying to scream, sucking in water. It was suddenly all there. The memory. The panic. Then Dad was pulling me aboard. *Don't ever do that again! Never!* he said. I screamed and he shook me. *Calm down, now. You just got wet. It's okay, it was nothing.* Then he hugged me. I remembered his arms shaking. *You're not a baby anymore,* he whispered. *It's okay, it's okay . . .*

Shelley kept quiet, watching me. *It's okay,* he'd told me. But it *wasn't* okay, it *wasn't* nothing. It was *everything*.

I slapped my hand on the hood of the Jeep, and it started to throb.

Shelley stood back, watching me. I jumped into the Jeep and started it, gunning the engine, hard. Then I let up and sat staring straight ahead. "Come on," I whispered.

Shelley waited a moment, then got in. Still silent.

I drove through town fast, with my eyes riveted on the road ahead, cold anger gripping me. I went two or three miles like that until Shelley spoke.

"Stop the Jeep. I want to get out."

I pulled off the road onto a stretch of dirt and slid to a stop. Dust surrounded us.

"What is it? Why are you so *angry*?"

I squeezed the steering wheel, my jaw tight.

"I don't know," I finally said. "I'm mad, that's all. I'm mad at Dad. I'm mad at myself."

Shelley reached for my hand.

The instant she touched me my throat got hot and closed, my eyes on the verge of flooding. Shelley moved closer and put her arms around me.

"What if he's dead," I whispered.

"Then we'll deal with it."

I laid my forehead on the steering wheel and started shaking. Dad—who I knew but didn't know, who could be dead now. He'd always kept his life to himself, shut himself away, even from me. And I had always been afraid to break in, afraid to even try. *Chicken. Pantie. Punk . . . afraid of the ocean.*

Gradually, my shaking stopped, and I felt drained, and strangely relaxed. I drove Shelley home slowly, and didn't want her to get out of the Jeep when we got there.

"Whatever happens, Sonny," she said softly, "we have each other . . . we'll always have each other."

When I got home, Grampa Joe's car was parked on the grass. Heavy shadows shrouded the trees under a clear, moonless sky. I turned off the engine.

The dogs poured down the stairs from the porch. Grampa Joe was sitting on the top step in the dark.

"You okay, Omilu?" he asked as I climbed up to the house.

"Yes, Grampa."

He stood and stretched. "Nice night."

I studied his ghostly shape. "Come inside."

He followed me in, squinting when I turned on a light.

"Hey," he said. "You still got that cat?"

I pointed back toward the screen door. Grampa Joe opened it and let Popoki in.

"Shee," Grampa Joe said. "That's one lucky cat. Whatever happened to that boy who wanted you to shoot it?"

I shrugged. "He went back to the mainland. Probably selling cars by now. He could talk you into anything."

Grampa Joe chuckled.

Why was he here? What did he want, anyway?

"Hah," Grampa Joe went on. "Remember the tidal wave?"

I frowned at him. What a time to bring *that* up.

"We saw the red truck in the mud and thought they were goners." Grampa Joe stared at the floor, shaking his head. "Raz and your daddy sure fooled us, didn't they?"

I waited.

Grampa Joe raised his eyebrows. "Well . . ." He started to leave.

"Grampa . . . Can I ride with you?"

He threw me the keys, then waited while I fed the dogs.

Grampa Joe slid over behind the wheel when I got out at Keo's house. The headlights threw a sharp-shadowed light over the porch.

"Omilu," he said. "An old man learns some things in his life about living on an island. I've been watching you a long time, all the time hugging the shore, keeping close to the land . . . and that's all right. The land is right for a man, just like the ocean. But your daddy's different . . . the ocean is his life, his friend . . . even if it hurts him . . . even if it hurts *you*."

Grampa Joe paused a moment, staring at the steering wheel. He looked back up at me and nodded once. "That's all."

He backed away and drove off into the night.

Not long after Keo and I had fallen asleep Uncle Harley shook us awake. I jumped when he touched me.

"We've got to get down to the pier," he said.

We stumbled to the kitchen.

The phone rang, and Uncle Harley answered before the second ring, then listened, staring at Aunty Pearl's fish tank. "Was it Raymond?" he asked.

Silence. Keo and I watched Uncle Harley.

"I'll call for an ambulance. We'll be down in twenty minutes." Uncle Harley hung up and hurried over to the ship-to-shore radio he kept in the kitchen. Static spit from it when he turned it on to listen.

My stomach tightened.

"That was Raz. The Coast Guard picked up a call from the sailboat that was here a couple of days ago, the one from Tahiti. They have a man aboard . . . found him in the water just before sunset . . . probably Raymond. Raz said the Coast Guard was still a couple of hours out. They told the Frenchman to put in at Keauhou."

I stood up. "Is he all right?"

"Raz didn't know."

The ambulance had beaten us. Two men in white shirts were waiting in the dark on the long, wooden pier. The small harbor was black except for a few yard lights from the houses along the shore. The running lights of the yacht bobbed in the distance, closing in on the mouth of the bay. I squinted out at them. It was just after midnight.

The *Moineau* anchored off the end of the pier.

The man on the sailboat threw in a line and Uncle Harley

pulled the stern close to the pier. The woman stood on the bow, the chain rattling through the hawsehole as she let the anchor out just far enough for someone to board.

I jumped on first, with Uncle Harley and the men from the ambulance following.

The Frenchman led us down the companionway into the dimly lit cabin.

I crept forward.

Dad.

He lay still, bare-chested with cuts all over the upper part of his body. And on his arms and hands. His right knee was red and swollen to the size of a giant mango.

The Frenchman bent down and put his hand on Dad's shoulder. For a moment nothing happened.

Then Dad opened his eyes and rolled his head to the side. He tried to smile when he saw me and tried to lift his arm. But a few inches was all he could manage.

The men from the ambulance pushed by and went to work on him, taking his pulse, whispering. Uncle Harley pulled me away, and together we went out on deck. Keo squatted on the pier, watching.

The Frenchman came up from the cabin with a large, barnacle-covered glass ball about the size of a small buoy. He pointed back down into the cabin. "Man . . ." he said, then wrapped his arms around the glass ball and held it to his chest. He handed it to Uncle Harley along with the net from Dad's boat.

Uncle Harley studied the glass ball, turning it around, picking at the barnacles.

He shook his head slowly.

I skipped school the next day.

I drove down to the pier in the morning and sat around in the Jeep until about ten o'clock, watching the charter boats take off and dozing. I'd told Dad I'd let him get some sleep and that I'd come up to the hospital in the afternoon.

I couldn't stop thinking about the dream-memory, how I'd somehow blocked it out of my mind. Why hadn't Dad ever talked about it? And I couldn't stop thinking about what had happened to Dad. Being left at sea, alone. Uncle Harley managed to piece the story together after we'd taken Dad to the hospital.

Dad was fishing in a school of porpoise, the tuna below. The school shifted and he put the boat in gear, on automatic pilot, and let it follow the school while he went aft to prepare his bait. While he was cutting a slab of *opelu*, he saw the glass ball that the Frenchman had given us just off the starboard side of the sampan. Dad ran for his net and reached out to scoop the ball from the water. He reached too far and lost his balance, fracturing his kneecap on the gunwale as he tumbled overboard. The boat moved on, slowly. But Dad couldn't reach it with his knee exploding in pain, so he pulled himself back to the glass ball and hung on to it. The hand net was still around the ball, and Dad kept it there. He said he would have been a shark's dessert without it. A big one came nosing around, but shot off when he poked it with the handle of the net.

He said he spent the night and all of the next day in the water before he spotted the Frenchman. "I was lucky I had the net . . . I waved it at the sailboat," Dad said. "At least the water was warm. That damn ocean doesn't care who you are or what you're doing. You're always on your own out there. Lucky for me that Frenchman came by . . . and lucky he wasn't afraid to sail at night . . . it was almost dark when he found me."

I sat in the Jeep until the sun got hot, until I could feel it burning my shoulders through my T-shirt. *You're always on your own out there.* Keo and Uncle Raz were out there now, fishing, as if nothing had ever happened, where they'd probably spend every day of their lives. And so would Dad, when his leg got better.

But what about me?

I wasn't one of them. I didn't *want* to be different. But I was, that's all. I didn't have the guts to be one of them.

I drove up the old road toward the hospital, a little nervous. What would I say? I thought of Dad chugging out to the grounds on a smooth, light-blue sea. There was beauty in that. I'd always felt that way. But I loved more the richness of solid ground—the meandering old bumpy roads and squeaky Jeep seats, the hot steel floorboard under my bare feet, the sweet smell of rotting mangoes, the hovering trees, the flickering early-morning sun spots.

And Shelley.

She'd be wondering where I was, and why I hadn't called. I should have. I'd been pretty hard on her. Was I getting to be like Dad? Was I closing down like Dad?

Dad was waiting for me outside, sitting on a bench with a pair of crutches, bandages on his arms. His doctor argued with him to stay at least one more day, but it made Dad nervous just being there. It was where my mother had died.

We didn't say much to each other on the way home, just talked about who caught what in the past few days. And I told him about our search, and how Mr. Pierce had been the one to find his boat heading out toward the other side of the world.

Dad listened, but didn't say anything about what *he* had been going through out there. It drove me *crazy*.

I knew Dad's silences drove Aunty Pearl crazy, too. I was feeling a little depressed one day and went up to talk to her. I felt empty, I told her. Dad and I hardly ever talked. She asked me if Dad had told me about my mother yet. "Only a little," I said. "You see?" she said. "That's what I mean. He hasn't even told you about the most important thing in your life, and his life. Nobody knows *anything* about that man, not even you. So many men around like that—living inside themselves. They're afraid to talk about how they feel, or even *think* about how they feel. But your daddy can't fool me. He's proud of you, Sonny. And he loves you very much—very much. But he has no idea in the world how to show you that."

The air got warmer as we drove down closer to sea level. Dad studied the ocean until the trees got in the way.

"Were you scared?" I finally asked.

Dad thought for a moment. "I could see the island the whole time."

"But what about sharks? Weren't you worried about them?"

"No."

I laughed to myself. What other answer was he going to give me, anyway?

The next morning I drove down to the pier before sunrise to take Dad's boat out while he was recuperating. I could catch up with school later. My grades were pretty good. But when I got to the harbor the *Ipo* was already tied alongside the pier, and Keo was moving around its deck in the light from the bulkhead.

I pulled the Jeep up next to the boat. "What are you doing?"

"Hey, cock-a-roach," he said, smiling as if it were his first day out on his own boat. "Getting ready to go fishing, what does it look like?"

"But . . ."

"Uncle Raz gave me some time off," Keo said. "You still got school to go to."

"I can catch up."

"Naah. Go. I can take care of this tub." As he spoke, he moved Dad's gear around to spots on the deck more to his liking. "But if you really want to help, you can throw me the line. Time to get going before all the boats get out there."

I got out of the Jeep and untied the *Ipo*. "Keo . . ."

"No problem, pantie. You're not much of a fisherman, any-way."

"I can fish as good as you any day."

"Sheese," he said, then shook his head. He coiled the line neatly on the deck, then went forward to the controls. He waved as he throttled up out into the harbor.

I sat on the hood of the Jeep and watched Dad's old sampan shrink to a black dot on the ocean. A burning rose in my throat and a trembling in my ears. I was grateful no one was there to ask me anything, because answering would have been too painful.

"You the cock-a-roach," I mumbled.

Dad, Uncle Raz, now Keo. Men of the sea.

Men of my family.

Damn bull-headed muscle-brains.

A week later Shelley and I built a fire in a sandy spot between the rocks, out near the ocean in front of my house, like Keo and I had done so many hundred times before. Uncle Raz had given me a fresh *aku* and I'd soaked it in lemon-butter sauce. We invited Dad out to join us. I wanted to somehow pull our lives together again after what had happened.

Dad watched us cook, his crutches lying next to him and his beer propped up in a rocky nook. Shelley and I stuck ice-cold Cokes in the sand, and the three of us ate fish and rice around the snapping fire. We talked quietly under a black sky. The surf hissed gently in, filling the spots when no one said anything.

Ever since we'd found Dad I'd been rehearsing what I'd say to him—I had to do something, our lives could not just go silently on. I thought of asking Shelley, but it was my problem. I must have been pretty quiet that week, because Shelley finally said, "You're getting to be just like your father, keeping every-thing to yourself."

"I'm sorry," I said. "I've just got a lot on my mind."

"Like what?"

"Dad . . . *Me* and Dad."

Shelley waited.

"I guess I learned something while he was out there hanging onto that glass ball," I went on. "I'm not on my own as much as I thought."

And what else had I learned?

That I wasn't one of them? That I wasn't like Dad, Keo, or Uncle Raz? Was that *really* it?

Who was I fooling?

I was as much a part of them as the sand was of the sea. The only thing keeping me apart was myself, how I thought about myself. Sure I wasn't as brave as Keo, or Dad, or Uncle Raz. But did that make me so different? Did that mean I didn't have any guts? Maybe only in my own mind. And even though I wasn't very much like *them*, I wasn't so different from Uncle Harley or Grampa Joe, or even Mick Pierce. *Your uncle is soft*, Aunty Pearl had once said of Uncle Harley. Remembering that made me feel good inside. No, it made me feel *great*.

After we finished eating, Dad, Shelley, and I sat around the fire watching our paper plates curl up in the flames. Dad's dogs lounged around us.

When Dad got up to go inside, Shelley poked me with her elbow.

"Dad . . . wait a minute," I said, standing. "I have something I want to tell you."

Shelley grabbed my hand and pulled herself up next to me. "I think I'd better get going," she said. "I've got a lot of homework." She walked closer to Dad. "I'm glad you're home, Mr. Mendoza. You scared us pretty bad."

Dad half-smiled, then looked over at me. "Go up and get the glass ball."

I got the glass ball from the garage where he'd been cleaning it all week. It was beautiful once all the barnacles were scraped off, an old Japanese fishing float, probably forty or fifty years old, and very rare.

I brought it back to Dad.

He ran his hand over it. "Give this to your father," he said, handing it to Shelley.

Shelley took it from him and held it close to her, looking down. She seemed to be thinking about something. Tears filled her eyes. She put the ball on the sand and stepped closer to Dad, then hugged him.

I'd never seen anyone hug Dad in my entire life.

Dad was as surprised by Shelley as I was, his arms out to the side, his eyes glancing over to me, then quickly darting away.

Slowly, his arms came in toward Shelley, then enclosed her. The two of them stayed that way for a few long seconds, then they parted.

Shelley disappeared into the darkness with the glass ball. Dad and I watched her until she was gone.

When no one spoke, Dad started limping back toward the house on his crutches, the dogs whisking around his knees.

"You remember when I was very young and fell under the skiff? When I got hit by the propeller?"

Dad stopped and looked back at me.

"I was terrified. I couldn't breathe. You shook me and told me it was nothing. I was screaming and you told me to calm down. You said I wasn't a baby anymore."

Dad waited, studying me.

"I was so scared I blocked it from my mind. I've been afraid of the ocean all my life."

The dogs lay down. Dad hopped all the way around to face me. "What's on your mind, Sonny?"

". . . I . . . It's just that I've been trying to hide that. I didn't want you to know, or Keo."

"I remember that day," Dad said. He was silent a long time,

leaning on his crutches, staring at the sand. "I was more scared than you. I was going too fast. When you fell off and I felt the prop hit you I thought it killed you. It scared me bad. I shook you because I was scared, because I thought I'd lost you, too."

The memory was clear, now. The nightmare, the gagging, the shredding life vest.

A silence grew.

"It was only a year after your mother died," he added.

Without thinking, I said, almost in a whisper, "What was she like, Dad?"

Dad dug absently at the ground with a crutch. "Wait here," he said, then hobbled back to the house. He returned with a book tucked under his arm. He handed it to me.

Anatomical Structures of the Dog. "What's this?"

"Read the name inside."

I opened the cover. *Crissy St. George.* I looked up at Dad.

"She liked animals, like you. She wanted to be a veterinarian, and would have been. I have two boxes of things like that hidden away. I was going to give them to you someday."

He smiled at me, a lonely smile. "I have always known that there is more of her in you than there is of me." Dad scoffed and added, "Lucky for you."

I held his gaze, and he looked back down at the sand.

"Don't fool yourself about me, son. I have hidden things, too."

Then Dad hopped around to leave. Even on crutches he was steady and sure.

"Dad, wait," I said. "There's still some fire left."

He turned, then slowly lowered himself to the sand. He motioned for me to sit next to him. The dogs settled down around us, watching the fire.

"Tell me about her, Dad."

* * *

At six o'clock in the morning three weeks later, I took Dad's skiff and headed out to sea. Two miles, straight toward the horizon. The ocean was calm, and as smooth as a fish eye. And blue—the early morning kind of blue you get in deep, deep water.

When the village had shrunk to a cluster of red and white dots on the edge of the island, I shut the engine down and let the skiff drift. Small slapping sounds squished out from under the hull when I took my T-shirt off. I couldn't turn back, even though no one would ever know—except me. I peered over the side into the thick, sucking, bottomless depths.

The fear started as a trembling in my jaw. My hands shook as I dropped over the side and swam away from the skiff until I was sure I'd gone farther than Keo ever had. Two hundred feet, but it seemed like a mile.

I stopped and listened to the crackling and snapping sounds of the sea, and breathed the salt-thickened air. I turned quickly and looked all the way around, pulling my feet up under me. Sharks roamed through my thoughts.

Slow deep-sea swells moved beneath me toward the island. I floated on my back and breathed with them, long and steady. I drifted for ten or fifteen minutes, looking up at the boundless sky, the ocean alive with its buzzing, yet strangely still.

A small school of silvery, inch-long fish appeared from nowhere and started nibbling at my skin. I laughed and rolled over. They shot away when I started back to the skiff.

The island was a dark silhouette as the sun climbed up behind the mountain. Below, near the harbor, specks of fishing boats fanned slowly out toward their secret spots on the sea.

A great peace rose from the depths.

WHAT IF THE WORST-CASE SCENARIO BECAME A REALITY?

Dylan's scout troop is camping in Hawaii where his
biggest problem is obnoxious Louie, a tough older kid.
But then an earthquake hits, followed by a tsunami,
and his greatest challenge becomes his own survival.